Dark Waters

# DARK
# WATERS

## EVEN SAVILE

*This one's for my co-conspirator and partner-in-crime,
Steve Lockley, who just so happens to be the kind of guy
I'd want at my side if I ever had to battle zombie pirates!
Buckle that swash, my friend.*

SUNBIRD
**PENGUIN**

Published by Ladybird Books Ltd 2012
A Penguin Company
Penguin Books Ltd, 80 Strand, London, WC2R 0RL, UK
Penguin Group (USA) Inc., 375 Hudson Street, New York 10014, USA
Penguin Books Australia Ltd, Camberwell Road, Camberwell, Victoria 3124,
Australia (A division of Pearson Australia Group Pty Ltd)
Penguin Group (NZ), 67 Apollo Drive, Rosedale, Auckland 0632,
New Zealand (a division of Pearson New Zealand Ltd)
Canada, India, South Africa

Sunbird is a trademark of Ladybird Books Ltd

© Deep Silver, a division of Koch Media GmbH, Austria, and Deep Silver
Inc. Larkspur, USA

Written by Steven Savile

www.ladybird.com

ISBN: 978-1-40939-0985
001 - 10 9 8 7 6 5 4 3 2 1
Printed in Great Britain by
Clays Ltd, St Ives plc

# DARK WATERS

# STEVEN SAVILE

# PROLOGUE

I've always thought of myself as something of a ladies' man, you know the type: a smooth talker skating by on a mix of roguish charisma, the odd scar and an eye patch to add that element of danger to the stubble and smouldering good looks. I'm not deep. I make no secret of the fact that I have hidden shallows. It works for me, what can I say?

But even my legendary charms weren't going to work today, more's the pity.

Of course, it didn't help that the object of my affections had been imprisoned for a thousand years.

The fact that I was here to kill her didn't help matters much, either.

That, and her being an ancient and eldritch being of immeasurable power and depthless evil hell-bent on destroying the world didn't bode well for the prospects of any long-term romance.

Then there was the whole tentacles thing. . .

It was hardly surprising my raffish smile wasn't melting her heart, really.

Mara rose up and lashed out, coming at us all writhing tentacles and restless malevolence as she shrieked and hissed. The bloodlust was on her. My left arm was cut. The blood was driving her mad. I looked at her. It was obvious she was intent on tearing us limb from limb in a vengeance-fuelled fury.

All things considered, I couldn't really blame her.

'Can't we talk about this?' I said. I couldn't help myself. I talked when I was terrified. Babbled, actually. It was a bad habit to go along with my smart mouth. If things were bad I could always be counted on to make them worse with a not-so-carefully chosen word.

Still, I wasn't stupid enough to stand my ground.

I backed up a few steps.

My knuckles were white from clutching the hilt of the weapon in my hand. Not just any old weapon, I reminded myself, the *magical* weapon that's supposed to be able to kill this thing. Seeing her rear up in front of me, transforming and changing, her body sprouting more and more tentacles as the temple around us trembled and shook, the mortar in the walls crumbling beneath the onslaught of her enraged screams, the whole magical thing wasn't as reassuring as it should have been.

It's not just me. Around me, the others shift from foot-to-foot nervously. For some stupid reason none of us imagined it turning out like this. Steelbeard blanched – which, let's be honest, is quite an achievement for someone who's already dead – and fell uncharacteristically silent, which was much more in keeping with the whole dead thing. Patty spun her sabre in her hand, over and over until it became a blur of steel. She took a step closer to me, winking as she did so. I smiled back. It was the grin of a man about to die, but glad to be doing it with a gorgeous woman at his side. Chani spat out some foul-sounding, jungle-born curse and glared in defiance at the approaching horror. A high-pitched yelp of fear and the sound of small feet scurrying rapidly away announced Jaffar's decision to *bravely* take up a defensive position far, far to the rear of our little party.

Gnomes: always such reliable and steadfast companions.

Can't say I blamed him, though.

The others stood their ground. They waited for me to

give the signal to attack.

I looked at each of them in turn. My friends. I couldn't think of a better bunch of people to die with.

'The time for talking's done,' Patty said.

She was right.

So close to the creature it was forged to kill, the weapon had begun to burn in my hands. I could feel it itching to draw blood. It wanted to *fly*. It had a destiny to fulfil. The entire length of the weapon shivered in my grip. Voodoo words swarmed through my mind, each one of them fighting to leap onto my tongue and have their magic spoken aloud.

Caldera, the Crystal Fortress, and my former life with the Inquisition all seemed such a very long way away at that moment. I'd come so far, learned and suffered so much, all to prepare me for this one battle. But all the preparation in the world would never have been enough. I knew that now.

The creature gave one final, hellish shriek and bore down on me, its tentacles whipping through the air with lethal speed.

I ducked the first one, barely, and brought the blade up to slash away the next, causing another hideous shriek to tear from Mara's lips as it bit into her flesh. It was a tiny victory. Other tentacles seized me, coiling around me in a crushing embrace as she lifted me high into the air. The world spun desperately, and I knew this was it, the end. And it wasn't the kind of end they'd write songs about, either. I couldn't help but wonder what final indignity the next few moments would bring; my body crushed in the tentacles' powerful embrace, my bones smashed apart as I'm hurled against the temple walls, or my limbs ripped off one at a time as the creature pulled me to pieces? All of them at once or one after the other? Not that it mattered to me.

This is what happens when you're an idiot and stupidly agree to try and save the world.

Again.

You'd think I would have learned my lesson the last time.

# CHAPTER 1

*Two months earlier*

Juan, adjutant to Commandant Carlos, commander of the Inquisition's last main bastion of power here in Caldera, knocked politely on my door and awaited permission to enter.

Well, when I say 'knocked politely' what I really mean is 'kicked the door open'. And, by 'awaited permission to enter' I guess I mean 'stormed in'. The heels of his immaculately polished boots stamped down hard on the stone flagstones as he delivered a well-aimed kick at a still half-full jug of wine and sent it sailing across the room to smash on the wall above my bed. It showered me with pieces of broken pottery and the stale remains of last night's cheap wine.

'Morning,' I said, groggily. It was a good guess and I had a fifty per cent chance of being right. It wasn't dark outside, so that discounted evening and night. I didn't wipe the wine from my face.

I supposed I should have been grateful. My quarters' chamber pot and its contents – considerably more than half-full – were only a hop, step and a kick away, and the temptation to choose it instead must have been terrible for the poor fellow.

'Compliments of the Commandant,' Juan smirked. In another life I might have wiped that smirk off his smug little face. In this one I could barely muster the energy to push myself up onto an elbow. 'He wants to see you in his office. At your *earliest* convenience.'

I stared back at him, blearily. My one good eye wasn't exactly up to the task of staring him down, being bloodshot and half-blind from drink. I guess that made me three-quarters blind. It took a minute to bring the world back into some semblance of focus. From the open door behind him came the faint sounds of marching and parade ground orders being barked out like the staccato crack of musket fire. Business as usual in the Crystal Fortress, in other words.

Business as usual, too, inside my pounding skull,

where a flotilla of Inquisition warships were firing off a full twenty-one gun salute in celebration of the sheer amount of foul wine I had drowned myself in the night before. I was a truly heroic drunk.

Juan looked at me, his nose wrinkling in distaste. It didn't take a genius to imagine what he saw staring back at him: an ill-shaven, one-eyed, broken-down wreck of a man who was, by no small miracle, a serving officer of the Inquisition.

'What the hell happened to you, man?' he asked, shaking his head. 'Don't you have any self-respect left?'

'Haven't you heard? I'm a bloody hero.' I started to sit up – or tried to. The ground spun alarmingly beneath me. 'I killed a Titan. Can't you tell? Look at all the glittering prizes that have been showered upon me.' I didn't bother trying to keep any bitterness out of my voice. 'I'm a bloody hero,' I repeated.

'Ah yes,' he sniffed, as though dimly recalling some particularly obscure piece of ancient history. 'That business on Faranga. Yes. Good job. Destroyed most of the place in the process though, didn't you? It's all been downhill from there. In fact, I hear we lost another ship to that Kraken just last night, right offshore of the fortress. But I guess you were too busy drinking to know anything about that, weren't you, hero?'

That caught my interest. My uniform was scattered around the room. I started to scramble about trying to locate the various pieces of it and get dressed. Come to think of it, I had a very vague memory of hearing screams. At the time I'd put it down to just another flashback to the hell of Faranga. All I had to do was close my eyes and I heard the splintering of wood, panicked screams and the symphony of disaster most nights. That was why I drank. Well, it wasn't the only reason, but it was one of the better ones.

I scratched at my jaw. I could feel the latest scar beneath the stubble.

'This got anything to do with why the Commandant wants to see me?'

'Who knows,' Juan shrugged. He was enjoying himself. Simple things please simple minds. 'Maybe he's come to his senses and is finally going to kick you out of the Order? Or with you being a hero and all, maybe he's going to pin a medal on your chest? Hell, who knows, maybe he's got a top secret mission for you?' And, with that, he was gone, laughing at his own joke. As it happens, though, two out of three wasn't bad.

'Let me get this straight: you're kicking me out of the Inquisition?'

The Commandant nodded gravely. 'I am. You are a disgrace to the uniform. You make a mockery of every principle the Inquisition stands for. We are mankind's last line of defence, our standards must *always* be higher than anyone else's, and our scrutiny of human weakness and its moral failings must *always* begin with ourselves.'

'When you put it like that,' I sighed. There wasn't a lot I could say. Not while my pores were still sweating wine. 'But you're also sending me off to the arse end of nowhere on some sort of secret mission that's liable to get me killed?'

The Commandant nodded. He was looking far too pleased with himself for my liking. 'It's really not that complicated. We need someone to infiltrate the pirates. He's got to be dirty. Someone they'd accept as one of their own. Someone desperate enough to turn his back on everything he knows because everything has turned its back on him. Think about it, who better than a disgraced ex-Inquisition officer? A hero fallen into moral degeneracy, drunk, debauched and so embittered with his former brethren that he is willing to throw his lot in with those scum? It's almost poetic.'

They weren't the words I would have used.

I was standing to attention – or the closest approximation to it my listing body could manage – in Commandant Carlos's office. Some people might have complained, cried out at the injustice of it, but my first thought since the Commandant handed down the dishonourable discharge was to wonder if that meant I could allow myself to slump a little because standing straight was taking up a lot of energy. We were like chalk and cheese, tooth and nail, or any of those other counterparts that just didn't seem to fit together. The Commandant resplendent in his uniform, me ragged in mine. His hair was steely grey, mine oleaginous black. One of his thighs was as wide as my chest. The same, but different. He gazed impassively at me across the wide expanse of his desk. It was a desk that said 'I'm so much more important than you in the grand scheme of things'. Behind him, pinned on the wall among various nautical charts and seals and banners of the Inquisition, was a map of the known world. All of humanity's dominions were marked out prominently on it. He didn't need to glance over his shoulder. He knew what I was looking at.

'Yes, not very pretty, is it? The northern lands – despite your heroic efforts on Faranga – are almost lost to us now. You might well have despatched one of the Titans, but unfortunately for everyone concerned four more of them still remain, and much of the northern lands are in ruin.' He shrugged. It was a *fait accompli*. 'And so we are pushed south, into these Southern Seas, forced to find new lands for our people.' He looked at me then, all artifice gone. 'We are clinging on by our fingertips, Lieutenant, and surrounded by enemies on all sides: to the north, Titans, and here in the south, nest after nest of those damned pirates. I won't lose, Lieutenant. I won't be remembered as the man who lost the world. But that doesn't seem to stop the world from hurling fresh crap my way.'

'The Kraken?' I said. I didn't say sir. He'd just kicked me out, after all, and wanted me to go deep undercover so now seemed like a good time to stop minding my 'Ps and Qs', even if he was still referring to me by my rank – ex-rank, I amended.

For just a second that impregnable sheen of self-assuredness that seemed to come with the Inquisition's uniform faltered. He nodded. 'Indeed. What do you know of the beast?'

'Not much,' I answered honestly. I wanted him to think I had my ear to the ground rather than my face in the mud, so I traded the one bit of gossip I'd heard. 'Some kind of sea creature, obviously. Preys on shipping in these waters. In fact, I understand it struck again just last night.' I looked at the Commandant, trying to read his expression.

'It preys on *our* shipping, Lieutenant. *Our* shipping. It leaves the pirate vessels unmolested. But not *our* ships. Cargo vessels carrying colonists and supplies to the outposts we're trying to establish, the warships and troop transports we need to defend those outposts, we're losing them all. That damn *fish* is bleeding us dry. We can't afford to let this state of affairs continue. It's as simple as that. Understand?'

'Completely. You suspect the creature is under the pirates' control, and that's why it is attacking only our vessels.' I was on fire.

'No, Lieutenant, I suspect it's under *someone's* control. There's a subtle difference. That will be part of your mission: find out everything you can about this creature, including who is controlling it.'

The bit he left out was 'and neutralise it'. I knew how his mind worked. It was all about reading between the lines. 'Right,' I said, trying to sound as confident as I could. Call it sixth sense, call it the world always kicking a man when he was down, call it Betsy and stick a bow on it, I knew there was worse – much, much worse – to come. 'And the other part of my mission?'

He leaned closer across his desk towards me, clearing his throat before he spoke. His breath was awful. I didn't wince. At least he had the good grace to look embarrassed as he issued the order that was almost certainly sending me to my death. 'The Kraken is a creature of sorcery. We have already learned to our cost that no ordinary weapon can harm it.' *To our cost*: that was how he described the loss of several of our finest warships and the deaths of hundreds of good Protectors, many of them my friends. 'Information has come into our hands regarding the possible existence of a magical weapon forged with enough power to slay the Kraken.' Magic. Oh, joy. 'Your mission is to verify the existence of this weapon, acquire it by *any* means necessary, and use it to slay the beast.'

'An *excellent* plan, *sir*,' I said, with all the enthusiasm of a man listening to his executioner sharpening the blade of his axe. 'And do we know the whereabouts of this magical artefact, or are we playing an elaborate game of hide and seek?'

'Antigua, according to our informant.'

Antigua. The most notorious and villainous lair of

piracy in all the Southern Seas. Oh, joy of joys. Every time he opened his mouth things just got so much better. So his big plan, apart from kicking me out of the Inquisition and making a traitor of me, was to send me into the midst of the Pirate Isles armed with a cover story so flimsy that the first wharf-front doxy I ran into would probably see straight through it without having to pull my trousers down. She wouldn't respect me in the morning, either.

I glanced out through the window, looking out beyond the parade ground and battlements towards the rocky crest of Gallows Point. That was where convicted pirates were traditionally hanged as a very public warning to all ships entering and leaving the harbour. I could see myself ending up there. Alternatively, to save us the march out to the Point, Carlos could just assemble a firing squad of Protector Musketeers, and have me stand up against the wall and let them shoot me right between the eyes. I'm sure there'd be no shortage of volunteers and it would save me a lot of grief in the long run.

'You really don't like me very much, do you, sir?' I said, not worrying about being tactful.

'Nonsense. I've arranged for our informant to accompany you. Her personal knowledge of these pirates alone ought to prove invaluable in your mission. She might even manage to keep you alive. Would I have gone to all that trouble if I didn't like you, soldier?'

He had a point, but right then the only thing I could think was: 'She?' I tried to sound casual, but I barely managed to keep the note of boyish excitement out of my voice. Any more than one word and I would have been doomed. *Surely it couldn't be, not here… Could it?*

'Indeed. A young woman, and rather a high-spirited one, judging by events surrounding her arrival last night. She was on the vessel that was attacked by the Kraken. She was found washed up on the beach this morning. By rights she ought to have been half-dead and confined to bed rest in the infirmary, but she's really quite remarkable. Feisty. A real firecracker. Even though she could barely stand she demanded to see me straightaway. Red bandana, good child-bearing hips… Now, what was her name. . .?'

He started rummaging around among the paper scrolls of messages on his desk, but it didn't matter. I already knew her name, and suddenly, the prospect of almost certain death didn't seem quite so bad after all. Hell, I didn't even care all that much that, for the first time in months, it was almost lunchtime and I hadn't had a proper drink yet.

'I believe her name *might* be Patty,' I offered.

I couldn't keep the smile from my face. Patty.
I wondered if she'd be happy to see me.

# CHAPTER 2

Ropes strained and creaked against the huge mast as the wind caught the mainsail, filling the great sheet and driving the ship towards her destination. I leaned on the guard rail, savouring the sea spray in my face. I felt more alive than I had done in months despite the fact that I had a raging thirst on.

No amount of water would slake it.

I needed wine. Good wine. Bad wine. Revolting wine. It all went down the same way. And beggars couldn't be choosers, especially when they were still horribly sober.

I looked out over the choppy waters, savouring the brine on the air.

It was hard to believe that this was the last merchant vessel in the Inquisition's fleet. Not so long ago they could have launched a task force to rival any to set sail.

The Kraken had damaged so much more than just the timbers of the old ship as it had wreaked havoc. I listened to the men's song as they hauled on the ropes, pulling together on each beat, while I looked out to sea. The song was subdued and lacked any of that camaraderie and *joie de vivre* I would have expected from mariners. Maybe they were thirsty, I thought to myself as I watched the water. I couldn't look away from the choppy spume just in case I missed some telltale sign of the creature. She was down there. I knew she was. Just waiting. I didn't release my grip of the guard rail as the ship bobbed and cut through its own wash.

Patty was born to the sea. She'd seemed one hundred per cent happier, and healthier, the moment we left dry land. I was already beginning to think she was part seal, or mermaid, for that matter.

'Relax, would you? There's nothing to worry about,' she said. It was the way she said it that got me, given the fact that the Kraken had destroyed the ship she had been travelling on and left most of her shipmates as corpses to wash up on the beach, along with the flotsam and jetsam that, once upon a time, had been cargo.

'You sound pretty sure of yourself,' I said.

She shrugged that annoying shrug of hers. It wasn't

so much devil-may-care as it was devil-couldn't-give-a-crap. 'Look for yourself. Commandant Sebastiano is hugging the coastline as tightly as he can. We're just off the rocks. Any closer and we'd risk running aground in the shallows.' It was true. I could see the way the wave pattern changed, signifying the treacherous water. We had a shallow hull. A bigger ship would have been in trouble. 'The Kraken won't venture so close to land, not when there's such easy pickings in the deeper water.'

'You seem to know a lot about this thing.'

She shrugged again. 'Not really. You just need to think things through: it lives in the water and it's *big*. Big things need big spaces to live, and that means the open sea not the shallows. It's not difficult to work it out.'

I loved Patty – in a 'there's no one I'd rather face my maker with' way – but in the space of about five seconds she'd managed to make me feel like a fool. That didn't sit well. She didn't even notice my discomfort, but that was Patty all over. She was the most single-minded woman I'd ever met, and she did whatever the hell had to be done to get what she wanted. Most of the time it was a case of just not getting in her way. Unfortunately, she wasn't exactly an open book. The girl liked her secrets. She wasn't in the habit of sharing her thoughts, or having big heart-to-hearts, and tended to keep anything she'd worked out to herself, so it was never easy to know quite when you were getting in her way. Thankfully, we were both looking for the same thing this time: I needed to find a pirate and she was looking for her father, who just happened to be a pirate. Steelbeard.

Given our relationship, and my quest, the stars might as well have aligned: Steelbeard was the one man who was most likely to be able to help me out. It all came down to trust. He had to trust me. And let's be honest, how better to win the man's trust than return the daughter he fears may be dead? Okay, I was assuming the story of the Kraken's attack on the ship had reached his ears, and everyone knows what they say about never assuming, but there was every chance that news of the *Esmeralda*'s sinking had found its way to Steelbeard. What I was banking on was the fact that it was highly unlikely he knew that Patty had survived the attack. It wasn't exactly common knowledge. Of course, it rather depended upon how many spies he had in the Crystal Fortress.

I sighed, the weight of the world somewhere just above my shoulders. It wasn't crushing down on me, yet. Yet is a very powerful word. There's the promise that it will happen, maybe not today, maybe not tomorrow, but some time before journey's end. But even now, with so much of the journey ahead, it was difficult not to wish that I had been able to go as part of the unit of men assembled and armed for the Fire Temple expedition. They'd been dispatched with orders to find out as much as they could about the magical Kraken slayer I was going to need if I wasn't going to end up as fish food. I tried not to think about that part of the whole grand adventure and just focus on the idea that there was a weapon of some sort out there… probably.

We reached the wreckage.

The surface of the water still showed the ghost of the ship in the debris floating on the waves. Fragments of hull and keel nudged against the side of our ship. Of course, I knew that the debris could have belonged to any one of the many vessels that had fallen prey to the Kraken, but that was sound reasoning and it had no place in my thinking right now.

The Commandant gave the order to trim the sails as the ship finished skirting the Sword Coast, taking her out into open water. Within minutes the sails strained, full of the sea breeze. The rigging creaked and groaned and I was glad of it. The faster we crossed this open stretch of deep water and made it to the relative safety around the Isle of Thieves, the happier I would be. That wasn't a thought I'd expected to have when I woke up to Juan's smiling face, that's for sure.

The short journey from there to Takarigua and the settlement of Puerto Sacarico ought to be plain sailing.

I hoped.

# CHAPTER 3

The signs of habitation were there for anyone who wasn't half-blind to see.

Actually, even half-blind, I could see it clear as day.

The thick trees had been cut back to claim what had once been forest, turning the land over to sugar cane fields. Some of the towering trees around the perimeter of the fields must have been hundreds of years old. Even now, they held some small amount of their nobility as they cast their shade. Workers were busy in the fields. It was backbreaking work. None of them looked up from their labour as we dropped anchor and lowered the landing boats. It was hard to understand why the Inquisition maintained small settlements like this, especially on an island where pirates came and went freely, lording it up on the other side of those ancient trees.

I had seen the sea charts, of course, and while I could see the strategic advantages of maintaining presence here – as staging point for shipping to and from Puerto Isabella, and even as far as Antigua and the mainland of Arborea – the cost of maintaining it just seemed far too high to my mind. Not that I was about to complain about its presence today; far from it. Trust and distrust so often revolved around circumstance and appearance, and how you sold a lie. In this case, it was going to look much more believable if I arrived in the pirates' enclave after seeming to have escaped the Inquisition rather than simply arriving by boat. There were always going to be risks, no matter how I went about trying to infiltrate the pirate community. It was all about trying to manage them. And that was where Patty came in. My life was well and truly in her hands.

'Welcome to paradise,' I said. Patty wasn't listening to me. I went to thank the Commandant for bringing us this far, and held out my hand for him to shake. He didn't. He looked me square in the eye and said, 'I hope you rot out here, traitor. You're a disgrace. But if you really want to thank me, see that rock,' he said, pointing up towards an overhang about fifty feet above the sand. 'Go take a running jump off it and let the tide take care of your corpse.'

'Charming,' I said. And in that moment I glimpsed my future. This was how it was going to be from now on. People would spit at me as soon as shake my hand. It shouldn't have surprised me but it did. I'd given all of my life to the Inquisition. I'd served them loyally, unquestioningly. I'd risked my life time and time again, and let's face it I was a damned *hero* and this was my reward? Suddenly I was worth less than nothing. That cut. Deep.

'I take it you have no trunk that needs taking ashore?'

'We're travelling light,' I said. It was something of an understatement. We had the clothes on our backs, nothing else. Patty because all of her belongings were lost when the ship was torn apart, me because everything I needed could be carried in the leather bag that was slung across my shoulder, and there was next to nothing in there. I'm not a great believer in possessions. They weigh you down.

I didn't bother with goodbyes. They'd slung a rope ladder over the side. It led down to one of the landing boats. Patty was already down there waiting for me. There were things I wanted to say to her; we hadn't really had time to get our stories straight because we were never alone. We still weren't. The sailors rowing us ashore might have been ignoring us, but they weren't deaf and they certainly weren't mute, so I couldn't exactly tell her the grand plan without giving the game away.

We looked at each other across the small boat, like people who'd done something particularly stupid, such as killing a priest together the night before and not knowing how to pretend things were normal come breakfast.

A grotesquely fat man with greasy skin, a handlebar moustache and a really bad wig greeted us on the rickety wooden jetty. It could only be Di Fuego, the Governor of the outpost. Put it this way, two men couldn't have both had such appalling taste in hairpieces. A short distance behind him, I saw a grunt in uniform. He was fondling the stock of his weapon, which, *double entendre* aside, indicated the level of trust (or lack of) the Governor was prepared to offer. This wasn't exactly the welcoming committee I had been hoping for, but, after the frosty goodbyes on the boat, it was the one I had expected.

'Pleasure,' the fat man said, holding out a sweaty hand. 'We don't get many visitors to our island paradise,' Di Fuego's smile looked pained, like a rat had just crawled up his backside and died in there. I shook his hand briefly. His grip was limp and his palms were soft. I had a golden rule: I never trusted a man with soft hands. It implied they'd never done an honest day's hard graft in their life. I handed him the letter of introduction. I hadn't read it, but the Commandant had assured me that it gave precious little away besides the fact that I was here to take Patty to the other side of the island. He read it while we stood and waited, hoping Carlos hadn't slipped in a line about me being a low-down no-good untrustworthy drunk who'd just been kicked out by the high command. There was a moment when he looked at me that I really didn't like, but then he looked at Patty and back at the letter. I could almost see the cogs whirring away behind his eyes as he tried to work out just who on earth she was that would require her to be delivered to the pirates. I wasn't about to tell him. I was pretty sure Patty wasn't either, not when there was nothing to be gained from announcing the fact that she was Steelbeard's little girl.

'I've taken the liberty, if you'd be so kind, to have a small welcome feast prepared. Nothing grand, but it's the thought, isn't it? I trust you'll want to stay the night, freshen up, rather than set off immediately?' There was a mild desperation to the offer, and I realised that he was a very lonely man locked away here. I could well imagine this posting was a punishment. The sun was setting over his shoulder. 'It's really not the kind of journey you want to be making in the dark. You'd do well to wait until morning.'

'I bow down to your greater knowledge of the territory,' I said, 'And, between us, a feast, no matter how small, sounds too good to pass up. Plus, I'm looking forward to a night's sleep where the bed doesn't roll with the swell beneath me, if you know what I mean?' I suspected Patty would have been more than happy to sleep another night being tossed and turned by the sea, but not me. I wanted a bed that didn't move and a wine glass that didn't slop unless it was because of my drunken carelessness.

It had been two days since a drink had passed my lips and my bones were crying out for it.

The food was simple enough, but simple or not it was by far the best meal I had eaten in a *long* time. I ate it like the condemned man scoffing down a hearty last meal. That was one of the things about the life I'd chosen, I never knew when or where the next meal was coming from.

'So, what's with this place?' I asked, filling the silence that had descended while we were stuffing our faces. 'I mean, what do you do here that's so important to the Inquisition?' The minute the words came out of my mouth I realised how rude they were. I couldn't exactly take them back, so I just brazened through them.

'We grow sugar. The plantation's a rapidly expanding concern. People just can't get enough sugar,' he rubbed his ample belly, emphasising the point in a way that it really didn't need to be emphasised. 'I'm the slave driver,' he grinned, and in that moment looked like some oily predator sitting across the table from me. 'I make sure we have enough workers to tend and harvest the canes, and break new ground so we can continue expanding. Soon, as far as you can see will be sugar canes.' I wondered what the pirates would have to say about that. 'Actually, you were quite lucky that we were due to take delivery of new workers. It's a long swim, otherwise.' He laughed at his own lame joke.

I hadn't noticed any workers on board. I thought about it for a moment. It was only a small crew. It would have been hard to hide away a bunch of plantation workers. 'I didn't see any other passengers?' I said. When he started laughing, I felt like an idiot.

'Why would you have? They don't let the slaves out of the cargo hold.'

'Slaves!' Patty gasped. She seemed genuinely surprised about the idea. I'd heard enough stories about natives being transported to the plantations not to be surprised, but I was still shaken about the idea that it had been happening right under my nose. I was at a loss for words.

'Of course, more often than not they're more trouble than they are worth. Only last month I had a stretch of jungle cleared to almost double the size of the plantation, and, can you believe it, some of them actually *dared* to object! The temerity of it, I tell you. They *claimed* the land was sacred to them. The mind boggles. They revolted. Can you believe that? They didn't just down tools, they picked them up!' His grin turned malicious. 'It all got a little messy, I don't mind saying, but we took care of them.' In this instance I was in no doubt that 'take care' was being used very creatively. He turned the charm on Patty, flashing her a seedy leer. 'A few escaped. They're still out there, but we'll find them, don't you worry your pretty little head about that.'

I thought for a moment that Patty was going to rip off a certain part of his anatomy that he hadn't seen for quite some time and feed it to the seagulls, but she was surprisingly restrained – like a volcano waiting to blow.

As the maid cleared away the plates, Di Fuego leaned contentedly back in his chair. He rocked it onto two legs as he dabbed a napkin at the corners of his mouth. It was a very precise gesture. Fastidious. He folded the napkin and set it down on the table. 'It's quite a hike across the island, you know. I can give you a map, but there are really only two possible routes you could take, and both have their own unique charms.'

Charms. He wasn't a believer in using the right word for the situation.

'Okay, let's hear it,' I said. 'No need to be coy. What are we looking at? Cannibals? Man-eating plants? Little bastard pygmies with poisonous darts and a taste for white meat?'

Di Fuego smiled ever so slightly as the maid cleared the last of the items from the table. He snapped his fingers and she returned with a map. He laid it out, holding down the corners with small brass weights. 'We are here,' he said, jabbing a pudgy finger at the South West tip of the island. I could see Puerto Sacarico clearly marked. I nodded. 'The pirates' den is here,' he ran his finger to the North East.

'Looks straightforward enough,' I said. I could see two different paths that snaked from A to B, and as far as I could see there were no remarkable geographical features between them. Not that I trusted his map to be remotely accurate. No doubt the big 'Here Be Dragons' warning had been rubbed out twenty minutes before we made landfall.

'This path,' he said, indicating the shortest route through the jungle, 'brings you perilously close to an encampment of escapees. We don't know precisely where the camp is, but our scouts have tracked the natives back to this territory. They're a troublesome bunch, regularly launching attacks on us.'

'Why don't you do something about them?' Patty asked bluntly.

'Oh, we have tried, my dear, believe me. We go after them but they disappear like ghosts into the night. I am merely cautioning you that if you follow this path there is a very good chance you will run afoul of these outlaws. Obviously, if I could spare a company of men to escort you I would, but sadly that is not feasible.'

'So we avoid them,' Patty said. She made it sound straightforward, but for the fact that I had never known her to avoid confrontation. Maybe she was mellowing with old age?

'Wise choice, my dear. Sometimes the best route is not the fastest or the shortest one. So, you'll need to follow this route, here. A lot less dangerous in terms of restless natives, you'll be glad to hear. Indeed, the only treacherous moment you are likely to encounter along the way is the old rope bridge across the cliff. It *should* hold up.'

The way he said it, I imagined he'd already been out and sawed halfway through one of the guide ropes, just to make things interesting. 'Native insurgents, frayed old rope bridges? I'm beginning to wish the ship had dropped us off on the pirates' doorstep.' Of course, I just happened to say this with my outside voice. Tact isn't my middle name. There was a stretch of coastline that would have meant a journey of less than half the distance.

'Ah,' Di Fuego said, clasping his hands across his generous girth.

And I knew he was about to launch into another list of so-called charms that would most likely entail swimming through shark infested waters, or braving flesh-stripping fish or face-eating insects in the borderland between sea and jungle. I didn't want to hear it. I raised a hand to silence him. 'I get it, the devils and the deep blue sea, no need to go into detail. If these are the best choices then these are the best choices and we make do.'

'You are a wise man,' Di Fuego said. I could have punched him then. Not too hard, just rattled a few teeth. 'I suggest you make your way to the outposts here,' he rocked forward in the chair and planted a pudgy finger on the map. 'If you have questions about either route, ask the garrison there. They are the ones who know the island better than anyone else and are best placed to give you the low-down. Now, if you will excuse me, I have to ensure that the new shipment of *workers* has been quartered. Very frustrating, but if you want something doing you have to do it yourself, don't you? Even the simplest of tasks.'

I knew Di Fuego's sort. They grew fat on the slightest bit of power and delighted in being able to subjugate others who had nothing. He wasn't exactly unique in that regard. Not even original.

But I decided against knocking a few of our host's teeth out just yet.

Tomorrow, though, was another day.

Anything could happen then.

We needed to be fresh for the early start, and I hadn't slept for two days.

I missed sleeping. I rather liked it.

The wine filled my head and made my eyelids heavy. Ideally I could have knocked back another flagon and really *relaxed* but I doubted the Governor's hospitality would stretch that far, and as much I was wanted to get really drunk I couldn't afford to sleep through tomorrow.

I woke on a bed that was much softer than any I had slept in before. It went beyond luxurious into pure decadence.

I was still clothed.

Worse, I had absolutely no idea how I had got there.

My head was hammering out a re-enactment of Faranga. I felt sick. I struggled to think through the pounding, and dredged up vague memories of another jug of wine being placed in front of me as Di Fuego left us. It didn't take a genius to work out that I must have drunk it all. I'm just a boy who can't say no.

'Wake up,' Patty said, kicking the side of my bed. I groaned again and risked opening an eye. She was armed with a bowl of water and I was left in no doubt that it was about to soak me if I didn't get my arse out of bed, fast. And maybe cold water might improve my temperament, but the odds were slim. I slung my feet over the side of the bed. The room spun around me traitorously. 'Give me that,' I said, my voice thick with the fur of booze, and took the bowl from her. I plunged my face into it. Water splashed all over the sheets and the wooden floor. It would dry faster than my head would clear. I came up spitting and spluttering and invigorated.

Patty stood over me. She had a disappointed maternal look on her face. She wore it well.

'What time is it?' I managed, rubbing my hands across my face briskly. My stubble was thick. More like a beard now than a shadow.

'A little after dawn,' Patty said, and then smiled as I tried to do the mental arithmetic and worked out the answer I was looking for was: *not long enough*. 'We're moving out now.'

'Now? The sun's nowhere near the yardarm. You're a sadist.'

'We go now, we've got a better chance of getting away without being noticed.'

'All well and good, but it might have escaped your attention, we're not exactly armed to the teeth. In fact, if you take all of your weapons and all of my weapons and put them in a pile we'd have exactly no weapons. I'd rather like to remedy that oversight.'

'That's where you're wrong, pretty boy,' Patty said, throwing a sword onto the bed beside me. I pulled it out of the scabbard to examine the blade. It was functional, wouldn't win any beauty contests, but would happily gut a murderous cannibal native if the situation arose.

'Where on earth did you dig this antique up?'

'While you were busy snoring last night the Governor came bearing gifts.' She patted the knife on one hip, and the vicious looking machete on the other. 'He thought this might come in handy, what with it being a jungle out there.'

'How thoughtful. Where is our charming host?'

'Still sleeping, I expect, or being bathed in asses' milk or fed grapes by a hundred virgins or whatever it is his sort do when they're not eating.'

The one place we wouldn't find him, I was sure, was out in the field overseeing a hard day's work.

# CHAPTER 4

We stepped outside.

It was still early. Far too early, really, and certainly far too early for my liking, but the one perk of the unholy hour was that the coolness of the air was working on the heaviness in my head. I was still feeling pretty damn sluggish but the pounding had eased. Give it another hour and I would start to feel alive again.

The fields were eerily quiet. A mist rose from the ground, the dew evaporating in the early sun.

Whether we actually succeeded in slipping away unseen or not didn't really matter; it felt good to be covering the first few miles without the clammy sweat of the full heat of the day clinging to us. A few hours and the high humidity of the jungle would make breathing a real labour, so any headway we could make now was good.

It wasn't long before the outpost came into view, as did the watchers on the narrow wooden watchtower walls. They watched us every step of the way, though they were obviously expecting us. Two men came down to greet us. There were no handshakes. They looked Patty up and down hungrily, and I assumed they hadn't seen a woman in a long time. I mean, she was sexy, sure, but she wasn't *that* sexy. They confirmed that the shortest path was indeed more trouble than it was worth thanks to the natives ambushing travellers. Part of me was curious to see if they would treat us with the same hostility once they saw that my travelling companion was a woman, but I wasn't about to satisfy it. There was the risk that her presence would actually inflame them, especially if we were travelling through their sacred land. Primitive faiths could be very strange when it came to women, and without knowing more about their particular beliefs I had no idea how they'd react to a woman traipsing through the holiest of holies. Finding out was a risk that wasn't worth taking, so the longer path it was. We'd just have to deal with whatever physical barriers were placed in our way, dodgy old rope bridges and all.

Patty stayed a good ten feet behind me while I spoke to the guards.

Her suspicion made me a little uneasy, but I said nothing until we'd followed the path deep into the jungle proper. Di Fuego had been right, the vegetation was reclaiming huge stretches of the path and my arm was *aching* from swinging the machete to hack it away so that we could pass. After an hour of this, I had to stop for a breather. I had a raging thirst, and downed just about all of the water the cook, Osorio, had supplied.

'So,' I said matter-of-factly, offering her the flask. 'How come you were so cautious back there?'

She looked at me like I was an idiot. I was becoming uncomfortably familiar with that look. She took a swig from the flask before answering. 'Look at me. No,' she said, when my eyes flickered over her body. 'Take a good look. What do you think I'm worth?'

'Worth? This is a trick question, right?' I thought about it. As far as I knew she wasn't carrying any valuables. I couldn't see any obvious jewellery and thanks to her unscheduled dip in the sea she was wearing second-hand clothes.

'Come on,' Patty shook her head in exasperation. 'I know you aren't the sharpest tool in the shed, but I thought that even you, with your Inquisitorially sheltered blinkers on, could have worked out what the biggest danger to me was. I'll give you a clue: I've already had the biggest escape I could have hoped for.'

I tried not to let my face show the emptiness that lay behind it, but it wasn't easy. Patty could see the glazed look in my eyes. She took pity on me.

'Okay, let's make this a little easier for you, shall we? Question number one: who is my father?'

I knew the answer to that one. 'Steelbeard,' I said. What I meant was the infamous pirate Captain Steelbeard, but obviously the rest of that was implied.

'Very good. So, think about it for a minute. I'm sure it'll come to you eventually.' Her words dripped condescension. She stood watching me, waiting patiently for the penny to drop. Ever the spendthrift I wasn't about to let it fall. At least she wasn't tapping her foot or drumming her fingers on my forehead, but her impatience was pretty obvious nonetheless. She sighed. 'Okay, let's pretend you're not an idiot then, shall we? How much do you think the mighty Steelbeard would be prepared to pay for his one and only daughter?'

'Ah,' I said. 'A ransom.' It all fell into place then, like tumbling dice, and I felt like kicking myself. I was grateful Patty didn't offer to do the kicking for me. It was easy to forget that she was the daughter of one of the richest men outside of the Inquisition. It didn't take any great stretch of the imagination to see why a lowly outpost guard might decide the gods were looking down on him, and what lowly outpost guard ever looked a gift hostage in the mouth? Even a high-ranking toad like Di Fuego would look at her with doubloons glittering in his eyes if he knew who she was. Hell, the richer the man, the healthier his dreams of avarice would be. It would only take a whisper here, a word there, and a plot would be in place. I got it. It was better to leave that world behind and find a place where she at least was safe, even if that was alone in the middle of a pretty unforgiving jungle with me.

'Okay then, let's get you out of here before I decide to cash in on your bounty,' I said, grinning as I started to swing the machete again. Patty grabbed my wrist, mid-swing, sparing the offending vine.

'My turn,' she said, prising the machete from my hand.

Ever the gentleman, I let her take it without so much as a grunt of chivalrous protest.

She started hacking away at the undergrowth.

I looked back over my shoulder. It was difficult to know if the guard could have seen which route we'd chosen from the watchtower, but I was fairly certain that nothing I had said could have given us away, even if they had known who she was with, but it was worth being a little careful anyway.

Ahead of me, Patty hacked and slashed at the vegetation. I watched her body with open admiration – but only because she couldn't see me. Sweat glistened on her olive skin. It broke and rolled down the planes of her shoulder blades. Her shirt clung to her back. But she was one stubborn lady. The undergrowth didn't stand a chance. She carved a path through it with grim efficiency, until she burst through, stumbling forward as the resistance was suddenly gone.

I reached out and snatched one flailing arm just as the ground beneath her feet disappeared, sending a shower of stones and dirt far below.

She screamed but I wasn't about to let go. I dug my fingers into her wrist as her feet scrabbled about, frantically looking for purchase. In that instant any lingering hangover was gone, banished by the blood and adrenaline hammering through my system. I stared into her eyes as she swung around. She kicked out. I absolutely refused to move even an inch. I stood rooted to the spot until she was able to scramble to safety. Gasping, she grabbed hold of me. I could almost hear her heartbeat racing above her breathing. I *could* feel it beating against my chest as I hauled her back a couple of yards so we could see what lay in front of us.

Somehow we'd veered away from the path, hacking our own one through the undergrowth. I could see the rope bridge a little way off to our right. While it may have been quicker to try to work our way across to it, it was safer to retrace our steps. It wasn't far, so we couldn't have left the path very far back. I didn't say anything, but as Patty turned back, I took the opportunity to check out the bridge. When Di Fuego had called it the old rope bridge he hadn't been kidding. It had been *years* since anyone had tended to it. Some of the wooden slats were missing, while others hung free on one side. It didn't instil faith in me. Hell, for a moment I began to think we'd made the wrong choice and would have been better off taking our chances with the natives, cannibals or not.

I followed Patty back through the broken stalks. It didn't take long to find where we'd left the path, and from there it was easy to reach the foot of the bridge. As it came in sight, I knew I should have warned Patty. I saw her face drop as she took in the rickety structure. She swore under her breath. It was a curse that would have made her father blush. She didn't break her stride, though. In her place I know I would have stood there staring at it, wondering how long it would take me to learn to fly. Not Patty. She didn't even look behind her to see if I was following, she simply said, 'Follow me,' and took a grip of the ropes on either side. 'But not until I'm on the other side. There's no way this thing will hold both of us at once.'

What she wasn't saying was that there was almost no hope of it taking the weight of one of us, never mind both.

It made sense for her to go first though, because she was much lighter and stood a better chance of making it to the other side, no matter how wrong it felt for her to go first. She could warn me where the slats were least likely to bear my weight, for a start.

I needn't have worried about her; she seemed to float across the boards, her steps as light as a proverbial feather.

She only faltered once as she stepped across a gap created by several missing planks in a row. Despite all of the creaks and desperate groans the ancient structure made, Patty made it look easy. She reached the far side and turned, waving me over. Even as I put my heavy foot down on the rotting plank of the first step, I knew that it wasn't going to be as easy for me.

The rope bridge lurched violently beneath me, almost sending me over the top and falling to the raging torrent of water far below. I wished I hadn't looked down. Nothing good could come from it. The river churned and splashed and roiled, surging towards the sea. It looked like a thin white line down there; I was so far above it.

The bridge creaked as I risked putting all of my weight on that first step. I felt the rope pulling at the wooden stakes that held the whole thing in place. I closed my eyes and took a second step. I was out over the chasm. It was all or nothing now. The bridge swung beneath me, lurching from side-to-side with my next four steps as I hurried forward. With the fifth, it swung violently. I had to lean forward and grab the side as my foot slipped through a crack in the boards. All of a sudden the river seemed like it was rushing up towards me in a vertiginous rush. The pounding in my head returned with a vengeance. My mouth was as dry as the beach. I needed water. Screw that. I needed wine. Lots and lots of the stuff. Enough to make me so blind drunk I could just stagger over the bridge oblivious to the hundreds of feet between me and certain bone-crushing death. We didn't have any wine. We had water. Or rather, Patty had water. She'd taken the flask across with her. The only other water was a couple of hundred feet beneath me. I wasn't *that* thirsty.

I paused – or thought I paused – for a moment, then heard Patty call to me. I hadn't realised that I'd been clinging on to the rope for a full minute while the bridge swayed in the breeze, creaking and groaning and taunting me. I could almost hear the ropes fraying as they strained to take my weight.

'You have to move,' Patty shouted. Her voice barely carried, the wind whipped it away. 'Someone's coming!'

That was all I needed. I was a sitting duck – well a trussed up one, to be more accurate.

I have no idea how she could hear anything. I couldn't. Well, nothing beyond the hammering of my heart against my ribs, the pounding of my blood in my ears, the rasping of my breath as I struggled to keep it steady and not give in to the overwhelming vertigo, and the endless bloody creaking and cracking of the rope bridge.

I took a step. And then another. I wasn't even close to halfway across. I expected every plank to splinter beneath my feet as I took another five steps towards the middle of the bridge. It swung ever more treacherously now. My knuckles were white, I was gripping the ropes so tightly. I didn't let go. I slid my hand along the rough rope, feeling it chafe against my palm. I would have killed for a couple of restless natives to smack about right then. Anything was better than this. I could feel myself starting to hyperventilate. I needed to get a grip, fast. I closed my eyes, trying to reduce the world to me and my next step and nothing else. It was a good job I opened them again when I did, otherwise my next step would have been into thin air. I was at the dead centre of the bridge. In front of me was the empty space left by four missing planks. I looked down at it. It was far too wide for me to step across, but somehow Patty had managed it.

Looking down was a mistake. A piece of wood still hung from the bridge. It swung like a pendulum beneath me. The river seemed even further away than before, but the rocks protruding from it stood out in stark contrast to the water. If I fell it wouldn't be the water that did the damage. It wasn't a whole lot of a consolation to think that I *might* be dead before I hit the rocks. That wasn't the kind of luck I was after. I tried placing one foot on the rope and using that in place of a wooden step, but the moment I began to put any weight on it at all the bridge started swinging alarmingly.

'Come on!' Patty yelled as an arrow whistled by my ear. It only missed me by a matter of inches. It was far too close for comfort. I wasn't going to be as lucky a second time. I cursed myself for tempting fate. Less than a minute ago I'd wished for a couple of restless natives. Yes, I truly did believe the gods hated me so much that they'd thrown some hungry cannibals into the mix just to keep things interesting. I'm glad I didn't ask for a flaming Titan, because, knowing my luck, one would have come reaching out of the rock face to crush me against the side of the cliff.

I tried to think.

That was a bad idea.

Another arrow fizzed by the side of my head.

Instinctively, I stepped forward, and almost went on a crash course in flight, but managed to catch myself before I fell. As another arrow came my way, I rocked back on my heels and propelled myself as far forward as I dared. I had to let go of the rope as I launched myself towards the next plank on the other side of the chasm – and right then it seemed every bit as wide as the gorge itself. My foot came down hard, square in the middle of the plank. This should have been great apart from the fact that it cracked beneath the full force of my weight and split in two, tearing at my ankle and calf as my foot went straight through it. The splinters cut deeply as I desperately tried to scramble on to the next step. I was already falling.

I kicked out in the air, making the bridge whip around beneath me viciously, which in turn made holding on all the more difficult.

Another arrow planted itself in the plank right in front of my face.

I recoiled from it, nearly letting go.

I thanked my lucky stars the archers weren't Inquisition trained, and their arrows weren't regulation Inquisition issue. Otherwise this sitting duck would have been a dead duck. That said, there's nothing like the fear of imminent – and spectacular – death to galvanise a man into action. The adrenaline surge gave me the extra strength I needed to pull myself back up onto the bridge as an arrow nicked one of the ropes above my head. I heard the *twang* of several of the threads being severed and the cords of the rope beginning to unravel along its length. The planks started to fall away beneath me on one side. There was no time to lose. I was up on my feet and running. The bridge was coming down. In a matter of seconds it wouldn't be able to support its own weight, never mind mine. The bridge lashed away left and right crazily beneath me. I didn't care. I ran. It was that or falling.

# CHAPTER 5

The natives did not follow me across the bridge. Not that there was much of a bridge left to follow me across. I figured they knew just how ridiculously weak the ropes were and had other ways to get across that didn't involve the imminent risk of swan-diving two hundred feet onto the rocks below. I could respect that sort of ancient wisdom.

Patty was already folding the map again when I reached her. She gave me a withering look as she handed the flask over. 'You really made a pig's ear out of that, didn't you?' She rolled her eyes and stuffed the map back into her bag. She wasn't hanging around. I couldn't say I blamed her; even if their arrows fell short there was something uncomfortable about having a bunch of headhunters wanting to. . . hunt your head, even with a huge chasm between you. 'Come on, not much further,' Patty said.

She was right. We reached the top of the hill, pushing our way through to a clearing. Below us we saw the beach, and beyond that, the ocean.

There was a four-masted galleon out on the dark water. It looked like a huge colossus, absolutely still on a shimmering sea. I couldn't see any flag, the sails had no markings, and it wasn't flying any colours. That didn't stop Patty from recognising its lines though.

'That's my father's ship,' she said, and I didn't doubt her for a minute. She started to run down the hill, as excited as a five year old on her birthday, leaving me to race after her. I'd never seen her like this before. Halfway down the hill she seemed to realise how she was behaving, and her usual self-assured veneer of detachment returned. She stopped running. We were close enough to the beach that it was only going to take us a few minutes to reach the sand.

The realisation of just how close we were spurred us on through the final downhill stretch. The path was still overgrown, but less so than it had been back in the jungle on the other side of the gorge. It slapped and scratched at our faces as we pushed through it. The sun was full in the sky now, beating down mercilessly. My shirt clung to my skin uncomfortably. Sweat trickled down my back, and down the backs of my legs and into cracks where I really didn't want sweat to gather.

There was a welcoming committee waiting for us.

Or rather, an *un*welcoming committee.

The moment we stepped out of the jungle, a semi-circle of polished steel and grim faces met us. They closed around Patty and I, sneering. I've got a thing about people who sneer at me. It gets my goat. I can't help it. I just want to wipe that smug look off their ugly mugs. I placed a hand on my borrowed sword, but even as it closed around the leather hilt I felt the pressure of something *sharp* dig in at the base of my spine. The man behind me made a point of jabbing the point of his blade again, hard enough to draw blood. I didn't so much as wince. I wasn't giving the bastard the satisfaction.

Patty placed her hand on my sword arm, preventing me from drawing my blade.

She was right, of course, drawing steel was suicide, the odds were ridiculous. Even if I could have taken a couple of the pirates with me, I wasn't actually here to kill them, and let's face it, killing anyone was going to make infiltrating their ranks a much more difficult proposition, even if there were a few unexpected openings.

'I spy unexpected guests,' a man called as he approached from the rear. I didn't risk trying to turn to see who it was. I could guess. There was an absolute confidence and command about the voice. The speaker wasn't someone who needed protecting. He was someone you needed protecting from.

'What should we do with 'em, Cap'n?' one of the men asked. I could see him running through the possibilities in his mind – possibilities that included grinding my bones to make his bread, and roasting my nuts over a nice open fire. He was a charmer. He didn't take his hungry eyes off me, and the tip of his sword didn't waver for a moment, it stayed aimed at my Adam's apple.

'Let me have a look at them.'

The gathering parted to allow us through. I really didn't want to walk into the middle of them, but the sword in my back prodded me on. So I walked. It was like I was walking the plank, without the water, or the plank, or the circling sharks, but no less dangerous.

This really wasn't ideal.

In fact, it was so far from ideal it was flat out bad. If I so much as coughed I was liable to end up skewered.

Danger makes me twitchy.

It also makes me babble.

'You really don't want to do that,' I said, looking at the sword an inch from a part of my anatomy I consider particularly precious.

'Don't I, now? Why would that be?'

'Well, considering I saved Steelbeard's daughter from the Kraken, I figure he owes me one,' I said, making it up as I went along. I really hoped Patty didn't contradict me. I know she wasn't the kind of girl that needed saving, but... I needed to have saved her if I was going to get Steelbeard to buy the whole hero thing.

'Did you now. . .? So where's my little girl?'

Patty pushed her way through the gap that had opened up between them, before any of the men could lower their swords.

It was a touching re-union considering there were half a dozen swords aimed at various soft parts of my anatomy. I was grateful no one got swept up in the whole thing and ended up skewering me.

'It seems you did indeed rescue my little girl. I owe you my thanks, hero. Doubly so for returning her to me, but excuse me if I don't shake your hand – or turn my back on you,' Steelbeard said, sweeping Patty up in a huge embrace. The man was a giant, thickset and incredibly powerful. He clutched his daughter to his heavy red coat, and then finally met my eye. That his beard was streaked with grey was proof of his identity, but the real steel was in his gaze. This was the pirate captain.

'What should we do wif 'im, sir?' one of the pirates asked.

I wanted to correct his diction. There'd be plenty of chance for elocution lessons later, I realised, as Steelbeard said, 'Put him in the stockade, Stipe, and keep him there until I've had the chance to talk to my daughter. Strip him of his weapons, but give him food and water. He *is* our guest, after all, just not one we want walking wherever he chooses, if you catch my drift. I can smell the Inquisition on him.'

# CHAPTER 6

As shows of gratitude went, it didn't. But I'd been in worse places and, for the moment at least, I had a full belly and nothing to be worried about.

Patty wasn't about to let her father to leave the island without at least talking to me, and that was the best I could hope for anyway. I didn't expect him to welcome me with open arms, the long lost son he'd never had. All I wanted was the chance to talk to him, and if I was lucky, convince him that I'd been kicked out of the Inquisition on my drunken arse and really wanted a chance to stick it to my old paymasters. I was figuring revenge was the sort of motivation a man like him could understand.

The cell I was being held in was comfortable enough and while it wasn't the 'light feast' Di Fuego had served up, I had been given bread, cheese and fruit, so rather than complain or sit about feeling sorry for myself, I decided to grab a little shut-eye.

By the time someone came to collect me, the worst thing I was suffering from was boredom. Though admittedly it was an almost terminal case.

The man who came to collect me carried a sword tucked into his belt, but felt no need to draw it, so I guessed that meant they'd decided that I wasn't an immediate threat to anyone. That was something at least. No doubt I had Patty to thank.

Steelbeard sat waiting for me on a bench that looked out towards the sea. His immense bulk took up most of the bench, leaving Patty to perch on the edge.

He made no attempt to move as I approached, so I stood facing him. He looked me up and down. His scrutiny was uncomfortable. I didn't say anything. He didn't say anything. Patty looked at both of us, and then looked out over the harbour. We weren't exactly a talkative bunch. I followed the direction of her gaze. Steelbeard's ship was the only large vessel at anchorage. A rowing boat took supplies to it. I put two and two together and guessed that meant that it wouldn't be too long before the crew were ready to set sail.

'Patty has told me *all* about you,' he said, finally.

I didn't like the way he said it.

In fact, I yearned wistfully for the silence of moments ago when anything seemed possible.

'All good things, I hope,' I said, but really what I was hoping was that she'd told him the story we'd agreed on, light as it was on actual detail, and not the truth, because I couldn't handle the truth.

I needn't have worried.

'Indeed. She tells me that she wouldn't have been able to get here without you, which is something. It seems I owe you thanks.'

'You've already thanked me,' I said. 'And, to be honest, I wouldn't have been able to get here without her,' I made a face. 'I'm not exactly welcome where my old paymasters have any influence.'

'And yet the Inquisition didn't try to use her as hostage, or bait, to see me swinging from a gibbet.'

'Because neither one of us let on who her father was,' I said. The lie came easily. He didn't seem to notice, so I assumed that meant I was in the clear, and that Patty was playing along with the whole charade. She loved her father, so lying to him couldn't have been easy for her. I owed her one. And to be honest I'd have quite happily given her one. But I had to concentrate. Lying wasn't easy. It took thought. The last thing I needed was to trip myself up on some stupid detail. 'Who knows, maybe they were more interested in seeing me off than worrying about what opportunities might have washed up on the shore.'

'Then I'll drink to your health,' the pirate said. 'But we're both men of the world, let's get down to brass tacks: what do you expect in return for this good deed of yours? Money?' He raised a thick bushy eyebrow questioningly.

I grunted out a short, harsh laugh. 'I can hardly go cap in hand back to those bastards, they'll have my head on a spike at Gallows Point. I was rather hoping I could barter my way into your crew. My good deed for your good will.'

'Hah!' the big man barked. 'Every pirate in the Southern Seas wants to join my crew, and do you know why they want to join my crew? I'll tell you why they want to join my crew, laddie, because I'm the best damned pirate there is, and they know they'll get fat and rich off the plunder we bring in. So, tell me, because I'm dying to hear what you have to say for yourself: what on the briny sea makes you think you've earned the right to join my crew? Have you even crewed a ship before?'

'No,' I said, honestly, knowing he'd call my bluff if I

lied. 'But I can learn.'

'Hah! I don't have time for you to learn how to tie a bloody knot, and I don't have room aboard my ship for men who can't offer something to my crew. So this is where we say goodbye.'

'I can fight,' I said. Again, I wasn't lying. Few were better than me with a sword. The Inquisition knew how to train its soldiers.

'I have plenty of men who can fight,' he dismissed me with an infuriating wave of his meaty hand.

I thought about punching him, just to see how well *he* could fight, but decided braggadocio was the better course of action. 'Not as well as I can,' I said. 'There's not a single man aboard your ship who could take me.'

'Well, he's good with his mouth, I'll give him that,' the man who had fetched me from my cell laughed. 'Want me to teach the whelp some manners, Cap'n?'

Steelbeard clapped his hands together gleefully and let out a great roar of laughter. Patty didn't look quite so amused. She had that *what-the-hell-do-you-think-you're-doing* look on her face that I'd come to know and love. 'Well, well, well, now this could be interesting. But I'm not sure it's sport, I mean, MacLaine's a brute, and you, well, you're positively *dainty* beside him. I'm not sure having you beaten senseless is fair reward for saving my little girl. What do you think?' I was starting to like the man. He was not the gruff and vicious pirate that he was painted to be within the Inquisition. He had a sense of humour, and somewhere beneath it a curious sense of decency. That was unexpected.

I looked my challenger up and down and up again. He was well built and solid, for sure, but I'd fought bigger. I'd also been knocked out by them, but that was by the by.

'I can beat him,' I said, hoping my mouth wasn't making promises my fists couldn't keep.

'Right, MacLaine,' said the Captain. 'What say you teach the lad a lesson in humility?'

The man drew his sword.

I looked at Steelbeard, then at Patty, then back at MacLaine. I was at a distinct disadvantage, what with him having a sword and me not having one. No one seemed remotely interested in redressing the situation, either.

So much for a fair fight.

I glanced around quickly in case there was anything I could use as a makeshift weapon, or a shield for that matter, but I couldn't see anything that would be remotely useful. I dropped into a fighting crouch, circling him warily. My best bet was going to be trying to disarm MacLaine and hoping that the lesson he had in mind was going to fall some way short of killing me.

Actually that was the only real advantage I had. If an opening appeared, I could take risks that I wouldn't normally have taken, because this wasn't a real fight, and the only threat was to my pride.

At least I hoped that was the case.

MacLaine closed the gap between us far faster than I expected him to. He was considerably faster than his bulk ought to have allowed, and surprisingly agile despite being several years older than me. I began to suspect I was going to be waking up tomorrow bruised and battered. Oh well. I'd just have to make sure I landed some good blows before he beat my brains out.

MacLaine took a swing with his sabre.

The blade slashed through thin air three inches from my cheek as I leaned back.

I really, truly, sincerely hoped he'd expected me to get out of the way, because if I hadn't the sabre could quite easily have taken my head off my shoulders. MacLaine laughed. I was the only one that didn't find the whole thing hilarious, it seemed. Even Patty had a smile on her face. I could have done without that, but I supposed it was all part of the act. I stepped quickly to one side, rolling on my heels to avoid the next slice as it cut across my belly. I barely got out of the way. The tip of the blade was less than an inch from showing everyone the fruit I'd eaten for breakfast. In getting out of the way, I'd put all of my weight on one leg. He leaned in and slapped the flat of the blade against my knee. Pain lanced through my body. I resisted the urge to cry out, knowing it would be taken as a sign of weakness. Instead I winced, and danced back out of reach, earning more laughter from my opponent. This wasn't going entirely the way I had planned.

If I was going to take his sword away I needed to get closer, but getting closer meant he got to club me around the side of the head if I wasn't careful. It was a trade I was willing to take though, *if* I could skew the balance in my favour. My mind raced. If I could lure him closer to the trees there was a chance it'd limit his swing, and maybe, just maybe, give me the opportunity to get inside and work on his body.

As my opponent drew closer again, I danced back, determined to stay just a single pace out of his reach, taunting him to come at me as I stepped back and back. It worked. He came at me, swinging again and again. The sabre whistled by my hip as he lunged, forcing me to sidestep promptly. MacLaine launched another blistering attack, sensing the advantage was there to be driven home. I stepped back and back. No one was laughing now. And then I was standing under the shade of one of the overhanging palm trees. This was it, now or never. Before I could do anything about it, my foot caught on a root and I went over. To anyone watching it would have looked as though I'd executed a perfect evasive roll. I hadn't. I'd nearly broken my neck. By the time I scrambled back to my feet he was on top of me. I jumped as he drew back his arm for the 'killing' blow, reaching for the overhanging branch and praying it was strong enough to hold my weight and at the same time supple enough to catapult me over the trajectory of his swing, feet first into his face. It wasn't pretty, but it was effective. Before MacLaine was able to react to the manoeuvre I had planted my heel in his jaw and sent him sprawling backwards on the sand. The sabre was embedded in the trunk of the tree. I left it there. To be honest I doubted I'd be able to pull it free and didn't want to undermine the victory with any sort of show of weakness. I dropped to the ground, and knelt with one knee on MacLaine's chest, pinning him to the ground.

He was out cold.

Steelbeard marched across the sand towards us, Patty two steps behind him. The pirate looked at his man, then at me. I did my best to make it look as though I'd planned the whole thing and hadn't just gone sprawling and gone arse over tit.

'It would appear that you have earned yourself a berth on board, champ. But I wouldn't want to be you when he wakes up.'

'Great. I could murder a flagon of wine,' I said.

'Wine's for girls, lad. You're a sailor now. The only drink that's crossing your lips is rum. Rum cures everything. Remember that.'

# CHAPTER 7

'It seems that my father is in some sort of feud with another pirate Captain who goes by the name of Crow.'

'We've all had birds who give us trouble,' I said, doing my best to keep the grin off my face so that Patty didn't feel the need to remove it for me.

'I don't know how deep the grudge goes, but it's not like him to nurse one quite so… passionately.'

'Why am I not liking the way this conversation's going, Patty? I get the distinct impression I'm going to wind up getting hurt. *Again*.'

'Don't be a baby. You're a hero, right? Crow's got something Steelbeard needs.'

'And my getting it for daddy dearest will enamour him to me forever, I suppose?'

'Something like that.'

Now that I was part of the crew, I was allowed to come and go pretty much as I pleased, even if the arrangement had only been in place for a couple of days. Patty came to find me without fear of our meeting being reported back to her father. Of course, that didn't mean word wouldn't get back to Steelbeard, but it was a little less suspicious than her coming to find me in the brig. In the two days since I'd fought MacLaine I'd learned one important thing: MacLaine was Captain Steelbeard's right-hand man. I guess I should count myself lucky he didn't hold much of a grudge. That said, I still expected to wake up every morning upside down and swinging from the yardarm with the words 'seagull food' painted on my chest.

So far, being part of the crew had meant I'd been kicking my heels, because no matter how often I had offered to help with work on the ship my new crewmates shook their heads and told me not to sweat it, they had everything under control. I found myself yearning for a crisis, just so I had something to do. Not that I needed to make trouble. I was just... bored. I'm sure sitting around on your arse day in day out wasn't what they had in mind when the tavern drunks sang 'A Pirate's Life For Me'.

But I kept my ears open. It was amazing what you could learn if people didn't think anyone was listening. It wasn't *exactly* spying, but I started to pretend it was so instead of being bored out of my skull I could *almost* convince myself I was doing something useful for the mission. The best lies are the ones we tell ourselves. So, I picked up a few tasty morsels of gossip, some about the place itself, some about the Captain. None of them came as much of a surprise if I was being honest. The entire encampment was run by a pirate who went by the moniker Booze, which whilst it was probably the dumbest name I'd ever heard a man willingly take for himself, was fairly apt, as his place in the hierarchy was down to the fact he'd set up the largest rum distillery in the Southern Seas. For some reason best known to themselves the Inquisition was turning a blind eye to it. That interested me, so I dug a little deeper. It turned out the reason was purely economic. Money makes the world go round. You need vast quantities of sugar to make rum. So Booze and his villainous brethren were happily paying a small fortune to the Inquisition, buying up their sugar cane stockpiles. And of course that bloated slug Di Fuego was right in the middle of things. The irony that the pirates were thriving *because* of the Inquisition wasn't lost on the men here. As an outsider I could see at least part of the bigger picture – the part with the Kraken destroying Inquisition ships while leaving the pirate's vessels largely unmolested. For every Inquisition ship that went down the pirates' influence expanded exponentially. I filed it away with the other junk in my head.

'So, did Pops just come out and tell you what he wanted?'

'Not exactly.' Of course he didn't. That would have been too easy. I didn't say anything. 'We have both been sleeping on the ship. It's strange. It feels more like home than anywhere else I've laid my head. I guess it's where I belong.'

'So you're getting close?'

'Yeah, there's an element of trust that comes with him being in his domain. He's king on that ship, utterly in control of every aspect of life. He's relaxed.' I could understand the psychology of that. People let their guard down when they felt safe.

'Many of the crew on board?' I asked.

'Not really. A few. Most of them are doing minor repairs during the day, but hardly any stay on board at night. They head up into the encampment to blow off steam. They know they'll be heading out to sea again soon, so they're drinking and emptying their pockets for Booze's girls.' I didn't need the visuals that thought gave me. 'That's why I was able to sneak into my father's quarters when he was asleep.'

'And?' I could barely keep the anticipation in check. Patty, of course, was enjoying my reaction far too much. She was going to make me beg for the details.

'He talks in his sleep,' she said, finally.

It took a moment to sink in.

'No way!'

'Yes way,' she said, enjoying my surprise.

'That's got to be bloody inconvenient for a man like him, babbling his secrets out between snores.'

'It's a good reason to sleep alone,' she agreed. 'He's tossing and turning all night, mumbling away. It's amazing he isn't a zombie during the day. The sheer amount of restless energy he's burning at night. He's sweating feverishly, thrashing about beneath his blankets. And all he keeps talking about is a curse.'

'Interesting.'

'I thought so, too, but when I asked him about it yesterday he told me not to be stupid, there's no such thing. It's all superstition and voodoo. Of course, we've both seen plenty of voodoo in action, so that's hardly comforting,' she grunted. It was a particularly *un*ladylike sound. 'I pushed him on it but he wouldn't say a thing other than I wasn't to worry my pretty little head about stuff and nonsense. There are times I think he doesn't know me at all. Rather than push him on it, I crept back into his room last night, and as the nightmares gripped him tried to steer his sleep-talking.'

'Clever. Sleep interrogation.' I could imagine a few Inquisitors liking that idea.

'Even asleep he wasn't talking, so to speak. But he did reveal one thing: Crow is the key to everything. He's hunting him because he has a weapon capable of killing the Kraken. Sound familiar?'

'Painfully.'

'I thought it might. Now this is where it gets interesting. By killing the Kraken the old man's curse can be lifted.'

'You're not kidding,' I said. 'So, we're all looking for the same thing.' I liked that. It meant I didn't have to steal the weapon at all; I just had to make sure Steelbeard did, and help him kill the Kraken and everyone would be happy.

Patty could see the cogs whirring away in my mind.

'So, we help your father lift his curse.'

'Do you think the Inquisition will settle for that? I

mean, they may *say* that all they want is to kill the Kraken, and reclaim the seas, but now that you're sober do you really think they'll be happy with the idea of some kind of magical weapon out there in someone else's hands? Let's not even think about the idea of those hands belonging to a pirate for a minute.'

'Not my problem,' I said. And it wasn't. Yet. I was really beginning to hate that word.

From the moment we'd set off, I had been working under the assumption that destroying the Kraken was the be-all and end-all of my mission, that the Inquisition wanted the sea monster dead. But Patty was right; killing the creature wasn't *just* about saving ships. It was about the way the terror was slowing down the building of the Empire and the weapon, whatever it turned out to be, would not only deal with the Kraken, but would be useful in handling any *future* threats they might face. Not for the first time, my paymasters left me feeling ever so slightly naïve.

'Really?' she said, not believing me for a minute. Sometimes I forgot that she knew me far too well. 'Then I suppose there won't come a time when you are going to have to make a choice between fulfilling your mission and keeping your word? I'm going to say this once, it's not a threat; I like you too much for that. It's a promise. I'll help you as much as I can. I'll be with you every step of the way, and together we will destroy the Kraken, but if for even a moment it looks like your actions are going to do *anything* to hurt my father, I will kill you.'

I knew exactly where I stood with Patty. She didn't waste words. She meant it. As long as Steelbeard's need and mine overlapped we were golden. I wouldn't dream of hurting him. And, I trusted, the same went for him with me. We'd cross all those other bridges if and when we came to them. It wasn't worth worrying about what happened afterwards, given that afterwards involved having taken down an almost mythologically powerful beast and walking away to tell the tale. That was getting well ahead of ourselves.

I was still pondering the possibilities when the bell on the harbour tolled.

'That's our signal,' Patty said.

I looked towards the jetty. Some of the pirates were already clambering into small rowing boats while others lined up waiting their turn to be ferried to the ship.

'If we're not down there by the time they get back, there's a good chance the ship will sail without us.'

'He'd leave his own daughter behind?'

'It wouldn't be the first time. I told you, it's been quite a while since we last saw each other. There's a reason for that.'

'You realise I am going to ask you what that reason is, don't you?'

'I'm sure you will, but I'm not going to tell you.'

'In that case, we'd better get down there.'

'It would be wise.'

# CHAPTER 8

Steelbeard made me swear an oath before I boarded. I didn't have a choice in the matter. No oath, no maiden voyage for me. It was only a few words pledging allegiance to the pirates, but it just tasted wrong in my mouth. Still, I spoke the words and we left the harbour silently. Little did I know just how important those words were going to become to me, or what a curse they were.

Each man knew his task.

Apart from me. I stood around feeling worse than useless as they went to it, hauling on ropes and trimming sails and doing all that seafaring stuff I had no clue about. We were well out into the open sea before Steelbeard addressed the men.

I got the distinct impression that this was business as usual. The men gathered round without so much as a murmur. If he'd asked them to sail into the jaws of Hell right then I had absolutely no doubt they would have done it, without question, such was the charisma of the man. That was the secret of leadership, of course. It wasn't just about being the strongest or the most ruthless. There was that X factor: that unknowable something else that set the man apart from the rest of his men.

'Listen up, sea monkeys,' he said, his voice cutting across the wind. There was so much power to it now we were on board, so much sheer authority. There was no denying his magnetism. He was their compass. They looked to him for direction. 'We are setting sail for the Sword Coast. I have heard tell that Crow is there and has tricked the natives into allowing him access to their sacred Earth Temple. Tricking gullible fools is pretty much what Crow does for fun, but there's usually gold – and lots of it – involved. He ain't exactly big on faith. Let's just say that. I can't imagine praying's right up front in his mind. He's up to something, and I don't trust him. So I'm making it my business.'

There were no questions and I wasn't about to be the one to break the silence. I'd fill in the gaps as we sailed. I hoped. The trick would be to do it without making it look as though I was spying on him. First off, I needed to gain his trust. People like Steelbeard didn't trust people who kept sticking their noses in where they didn't belong. So if no one else was asking questions, then silence and ignorance would be my disguise.

Steelbeard looked at his men one at a time, holding each pair of eyes for a moment. 'If we don't stop him, whatever it is that he's doing, it could be disastrous for all of us. We have a good way of life right now, and I'm not inclined to let anything threaten it. So, my friends, I ask you one question: are you with me?'

There was a great cry of, 'Aye' from the assembled throng as the men raised their cutlasses and sabres into the air. I hadn't got my sword back, so, caught up in the euphoria of the moment I punched the air with my fist in salute to the man. The cry went up again and again, steel clashing on steel and feet stamping on the decking until it became a riotous cacophony. Surely it was loud enough to rouse the Kraken?

Beside me, Patty stamped her feet.

'He's quite something isn't he?' she said. I could barely hear her, and no one else was listening. They were watching the Captain in case he had anything more to say before they set to work. As the cheers died down, he held up his hand for quiet. He was a magician. With one gesture silence fell.

'I'll tell you true, my friends, this voyage may not bring you riches, and it won't keep your bed warm with ample breasted women, *but* if we succeed in stopping this traitor, then I pledge to you all here and now that I will pay a bounty to every man who sails with me, and to any man who falls before journey's end I will pay double to their family. If I die then my daughter will make sure that my wishes are carried out.'

There was more cheering, only slightly less raucous this time, and one or two of the pirates risked a furtive glance Patty's way. It was highly unlikely they'd been unaware of who she was, news travelled fast after all, but this was the first time some of them had set eyes on her. The effect was like some powerful enchantment. More than a dozen men fell in love at that moment, and would have done anything to gain the favour of the Captain's daughter. In return, Patty managed a rather forced smile, nodding vaguely to acknowledge their attention, but no more than that.

And then the gathering was over as Steelbeard clapped his hands and gave the order for the men to get back to work. In a matter of moments, life on the ship returned to the kind of normality I'd been expecting as the sailors dispersed to the four corners of the galleon. I had no idea what I was supposed to do, only that I was meant to report to MacLaine. It was the first time I'd talked to him since I'd beaten him senseless in the fight.

I wasn't looking forward to it.

I needn't have worried; the pirate greeted me like a long lost friend. He wrapped an arm around my shoulder, laughing off the boot to the jaw like it was nothing. Maybe it was. I had no idea how thick his skull was. Or maybe I'd earned his respect. Some people were strange like that. They admired those who could kick the crap out of them. The thing was, without tripping over my own feet there was no way I would have won our little duel, but if he knew that, at least he wasn't letting on. I just thanked my lucky stars that there was no sign of enmity or festering anger. Given that we were about to spend weeks living on top of each other, with nowhere to go to get out of each other's faces except overboard, I was grateful to have one less thing to worry about.

'So, you've never worked on board a ship before then, laddie?' MacLaine asked. He didn't wait for an answer. I guess it showed in my slightly seasick complexion. 'But, if I recall you've got a good pair of dancing feet, so how about you make yourself useful and take a turn in the crow's nest.' He jabbed a finger up towards the top of the main mast as though I needed telling where the crow's nest might be found. I didn't. There weren't that many birds that made their nests down on the safety of the ground, after all.

MacLaine pulled a rope free for me, and held it out helpfully, waiting for me to start my ascent.

I looked up at the basket. It was an awfully long way up. I'd never given a second thought to how the lookout was supposed to climb up to the highest point on the ship. Mercifully I'd had a childhood full of tree houses and cliffs and generally risking life and limb over precarious drops. I suspected that MacLaine was hoping for a chance to get one over on me, but as I grasped the rope and shimmied up it, he did well to hide his disappointment.

There was a strange freedom that came with being up there, above everyone else, looking down on the churning waves. I closed my eyes, savouring the chill wind on my face. It was curiously even more exhilarating a feeling than standing at the eye of a storm as the hurricane whipped up, or spurring a powerful warhorse into a flat out gallop, both of which I had done. I felt every single pitch and roll of the ship as it dipped in and out of the waves, ploughing through the sea, every movement exaggerated by the sheer dizzying height of the mast.

When I opened my eyes and looked down again the crew were like ants marching between crates and coils of rope, each moving with a purpose.

The likelihood of seeing an Inquisition ship on the open sea was much smaller now than it had been even a few months ago, thanks mainly to the fact that the Kraken had decimated the fleet. It was hardly surprising that an element of caution had crept in. So, the chances were that any sails would belong to other pirate ships, meaning they didn't pose a threat, which just felt wrong to me. Still, it meant I could keep an eye out for any telltale ripples or bubbles or whatever else might give away the presence of the Kraken lurking down there.

I couldn't take my eyes off the water.

It was hypnotic.

The solitude gave me time to think about the pirates' existence, and just how much they needed the Inquisition. Actually, just how much they needed each other. It was a perfect symbiotic relationship: the pirates needed someone to prey on while the Inquisition needed a threat to be seen to fight against, otherwise it was hard to justify their military order if it wasn't needed to maintain peace and the illusion of safety. I'd been a pirate only a couple of days, and already I was beginning to doubt everything I'd been taught. The fact was, living amidst them, it didn't take a genius to realise that, without the other, both sides would have to question the fundamental purpose of their existence. I'm not sure either group were ready to get existential quite yet.

After six hours up there in the crow's nest though, I was less enamoured with the view. Every muscle ached, even ones I wasn't aware I had, and I was thoroughly miserable and desperate to be able to walk more than two steps in one direction. I'd forgotten what it was like to stretch my legs. When the shift bell sounded, signifying the end of my watch, I almost cried out with joy. Then I realised I was going to have to get down the rope. Getting up had been bad enough, but thoroughly exhausted, muscles knotted up in cramps, I just couldn't stretch out no matter how much I tried. Getting down again was nothing short of pure agony.

No wonder accidents happened.

# CHAPTER 9

'Land ahoy!'
It wasn't my shout. Despite having put plenty of hours in up in the crow's nest, the first sight of the Sword Coast fell to Stipe, who was serving as lookout. To be honest, I doubt I'd have been able to see it as soon as he had. I leaned out over the guard rail, peering in the general direction of where Stipe was indicting the land should lie. I couldn't see anything but waves and more waves, and beyond them, yep, even more waves.

The Captain emerged from his cabin, scowled into the sun and raised a small brass telescope to one eye, scanning the horizon with it before barking orders to MacLaine. We were almost there and a mixture of nervous tension and excitement quickly spread through the crew; atmospheres can be like that, contagious, or a contagion.

I wasn't getting swept up in their enthusiasm this time. I looked for Patty but didn't see her. Sailors took up their positions. No matter what I'd been told about pirates, this lot were every bit as disciplined as any Inquisition force I'd watched do their drills. It was impressive.

But no amount of drills could have prepared us for what happened next.

As we began to draw closer, I saw a single ship berthed in the harbour. Word spread like wildfire through the crew: it was Captain Crow's ship. I couldn't tell one ship from another, but the men around me lived and died by their knowledge of the seas, and the vessels that sailed on her. If they said it was Crow's, it was Crow's. And any doubt there had been about us catching up with him in this inhospitable arse-end of the world were banished, just like that.

'Any signs of life?' Steelbeard called up to the man in the crow's nest. Stipe polished the end of his spyglass, and then leaned dangerously forward, almost to the point of toppling out of the basket, as he took the time to survey the lie of the land.

'A handful of locals,' he called down. 'No sign of white skin, pink skin, or any variety of blistered or sunburned skin in-between. Meaning no sign of Crow's crew, Cap'n.'

Steelbeard sniffed sharply, his brow furrowing. I had noticed that he had a habit of teasing out a single grey hair from his beard when he was deep in thought. 'So, that means one of a few things. They've either not noticed our approach, which is unlikely, or don't see us as a threat, which is insulting–'

'Or they're waiting to spring an ambush on us the moment we go ashore,' I muttered, a little more loudly than I had intended. And of course it was just my luck that the wind chose that precise moment to drop to a murmur, so that every man and his scurvy dog heard me interrupt Steelbeard.

The pirate captain looked at me.

I thought for one moment he was going to backhand me across the jaw, but then he simply nodded, once, curtly. 'Our new *friend* is of course quite correct,' he said. 'And that is why he will lead the landing party to investigate.' He looked at me then, mischief glittering in his dark eyes. Great. I'd pissed the pirate captain off, so now he was feeding me to the enemy. Bloody marvellous. That was right up there with winding up a Titan on the list of dumb things I'd done recently. But I couldn't exactly argue about it, could I? Not without looking like a total coward.

So I simply nodded back, accepting the charge. Steelbeard explained his reasoning, and managed to make it sound like he wasn't being a petty little no mark, even though we all knew he was. I'd made the mistake of interrupting him, and for that I had to be put firmly back in my place. 'I want you to listen to what he says. Remember, he isn't like us. He's trained in the ways of the Inquisition.' He made it sound like I was some sort of pervert. 'And that single thing may well be the deciding factor that tips this whole affair in our favour. Crow thinks he knows how I think, and because of that, thinks he knows what he needs to do to counter what I would do. He won't be expecting the Inquisition.'

No one does, I thought.

I had to look at it this way: I was being given a chance to prove myself once and for all. Take down Crow's ambush, earn the big man's trust once and for all. I knew I was the most expendable member of the crew as far as Steelbeard was concerned, it was painfully obvious, no matter how much Patty liked me. So it was a win-win for him. If I fell victim to Crow's welcoming committee, I'd served my purpose and no tears would be shed. And if I didn't? Well, then I lived to fall another day. Like I said, win-win.

Steelbeard gave the order, 'Mister MacLaine, if you'd be so kind as to assemble a landing party.'

The men who joined me in the landing boat didn't seem best pleased by my company. I was the outsider after all, and maybe, like Steelbeard, they could still smell the Inquisition on me. They couldn't have been all that enthusiastic about taking orders from me given that none of them knew me or what kind of man I'd be when it was backs to the wall time. I couldn't really blame them. I mean, I had one eye. That suggested at least one lapse of judgement that had almost wound up getting me killed. Add that to the whole "tainted by the touch of the Inquisition thing" and the shuffling bums on seats shouldn't have been all that surprising.

There was no sign of Crow or any of his men as we disembarked. Actually, there was no one even remotely interested in our arrival. O'Brian, the ship's cook, Blake, a bit of a brawler, Morris and Gruff each drew their swords. I drew mine. This was my team. I was grateful to finally have my hand wrapped around the hilt, and as we made our way up the beach, I gave the signal and we moved fast and low, legs pumping furiously, churning sand as we tried to keep as close to the line of trees as we could. The sun was up, so we couldn't exactly slip ashore unnoticed, but we could reduce the chance of being seen by unwanted eyes.

Halfway up the beach I caught sight of movement in the trees. A figure started to run. So, Crow had planted spies, then. The man took off like a rabbit. The chances of catching up with him were slim, but I wasn't about to let him deliver his report to Crow if a few minutes exertion could buy us the element of surprise. Even if Crow knew we were coming, he didn't know how many of us there were. I wanted to keep it that way.

I pushed through the trees, branches whipping at my face and tearing at my clothes.

He stuck to the beaten path, which helped, but not as much as the fact he'd slowed down once he thought he was away. I hared after him, closing the gap quickly and praying that I wouldn't hit a sinkhole, a set, warren or tree root. He didn't realise I was there until it was too late for him to do anything about it – because I was on his back and dragging him down to the leafy ground. We both went sprawling. I straddled the man and hauled him around. When I had him on his back I had to do a double take: he was most definitely, and defiantly, a she.

'Ah, I turn my back for a moment and what do you do? Run off with another woman?' Patty shook her head in mock-exasperation as she came up behind me. 'And to think I gave you my most precious gift.' She fingered the tip of her knife, smiling wickedly before she burst out laughing.

The woman took a moment to think about the joke. Maybe it was my weight on her stomach or the fact that my sword was digging into her hip, but she began to laugh, too. She didn't seem to pose a huge threat at that moment, apart from to my ego. I felt my grip on her arms relax. Only slightly, but it was enough for her.

She titled her head away from me, hawked and spat. She looked back up at me. All I can remember seeing was white teeth: lips peeled back on pearly white. 'You're not with the pirates?' she asked. She had a way of looking at me that was uncomfortable, like her eyes were stripping away the layers of me behind my eyes, all the little barriers I put up to hide the real man. She looked through the drunk, through the hero, through the fool, to the man buried away at the bottom. Even I hadn't seen him for years.

'You'll have to be more precise,' I said.

'Crow's men. You are not with them?'

I shook my head. 'Nothing to do with him,' I said. 'We're with Steel–' Patty coughed right across her father's name, making it impossible for the girl to hear. I should have thought about that myself, rather than just give the game away because a gorgeous woman was under me; but I'm a guy, we do dumb things when we've got women on their backs beneath us. 'As a matter of fact, I thought you might have been Crow's eyes sent to watch for us.'

'She still could be,' Patty said, the only one of us not thinking with her nether regions.

The woman shook her head. Beauty is in the eye of the beholder, and I was beholding. I was beholding a lot. Her hood had fallen back around her shoulders, revealing tight black curls cropped close to her skull boyishly, but there was nothing else boyish about her. She had a thick white band of paste drawn across her nose and cheeks, like a mask, and a circle that could have been a third-eye painted in the middle of her forehead, but I wasn't looking at any of that. She had the most incredible dusky skin, dark soulful eyes and lips I could have lost myself in for days, never mind hours. I realised I was staring, but decided to brazen it out. She barked out a bitter laugh. So bitter was it, I couldn't help but wonder what Crow had ever done to her. 'They are in the temple – all of them save for three left to guard the ship. When I saw your ship approach I feared that you were reinforcements come to join them.'

'We're not,' I assured her.

Patty wasn't interested in offering any reassurances; she wanted answers. 'What are they doing in the temple?'

The woman's face twisted, turning ugly as revulsion crossed it. 'That bastard Crow has tricked my father into letting him in there,' she spat. I had no doubt it was true. You couldn't feign that level of hatred convincingly.

'That doesn't answer my question,' Patty pressed her.

The woman shifted beneath me. I thought for a moment she was going to throw me off. She didn't. She turned to meet Patty's eyes. There was open hostility there. She didn't trust us in the slightest – but then, I can't imagine I'd have been too trusting in her place. Pirates invade her home and force their way into her scared temple, threatening her father in the process, and then more pirates show up and claim to be the good guys. Yeah, I wouldn't have bought it, either. 'I believe Crow intends to harness the power of the sacred temple and use it to unleash the Earth Titan.'

Oh, crap.

I knew things had been going too well.

I wasn't the kind of guy who got to enjoy a quiet life. There'd be no dying in my sleep at the ripe old age of one hundred and eleven for me.

I looked at Patty.

She looked at me.

I wanted to scream.

She gave me that look – the one that said I was going to get hurt, a lot, in the very near future. She had psychic moments did Patty.

'The Earth Titan?' I said. It was a pretty redundant thing to say. I was already wondering how I could turn back time about a week and, on my do-over, play dead this time when Juan came knocking. I fingered my eyepatch. I'd noticed I'd started doing that when I was uncomfortable.

The woman looked at me like I was stupid. 'That's what I said. Do you want to let me up, or are you enjoying yourself there too much?'

I clambered off her, and held out a hand to help her up from the forest floor. I was on guard for any sudden moves, a lunge and a dagger to the gut, or a slice to the calves to cripple. She took my hand and stood.

'My name is Chani,' she said. 'I am the daughter of

the tribe. My father is the chieftain. Or he was before he fell under the Crow's spell. Now I do not know what he is… a puppet with someone else pulling his strings. They have cast a spell on him, they *must* have. He would not be so foolish otherwise. I can't believe he would willingly be a party to this stupidity.'

I looked at her. In a few words the situation had gone from bad to worse to oh my god what am I thinking? 'Controlling him, how?'

'Voodoo. I have seen that look many times on victims of the art. The emptiness behind the eyes. The hunger in that void. It sucks out the soul and replaces it with something else… the will of another. And before you say 'stupid girl' and try to tell me I have it wrong, believe me, I am not wrong. I am no stupid child. I have studied the art for most of my life. I am a gifted practitioner. I *know* the look of a man who is being controlled by another. I know it, because I have done it.' I really didn't like the sound of that. A woman capable of making you do her bidding wasn't exactly an alien concept. I'd done plenty of dumb things because a woman wanted me to. But not because of magic. At least I didn't think so. There's no telling though with some women. 'And he is not the only one. It is like a disease he has caught from the pirate.'

That surprised me. I hadn't considered the notion that Crow could be acting under the influence. Actually, I hadn't considered much beyond finding the weapon, and making like a shepherd and getting the flock out of there. I wasn't sure I wanted to consider the implications, but I asked the question anyway: 'Who could be controlling them?'

I didn't expect an answer, especially not from Patty.

'Mara,' she said the name with surprising conviction. I looked at her. The voodoo woman, Chani, looked as though she'd been slapped across that beautiful face of hers. Patty stood fiercely defiant between the pair of us. She planted her hands on her hips. Sniffed.

'And that would be? Who? Precisely?' I asked.

'My father believes that Crow may be working for the sea demon, Mara.'

'More sleep talk?'

She nodded.

'You know, it might have been good to hear that little nugget of information a little sooner.'

'Would it have made any difference?'

I shrugged. 'Probably not, but it just makes me wonder what else you aren't telling me, you know?'

She gave me a look then that could have punctured

my lung. 'You think I am lying to you?' I shook my head quickly. 'Well, I'm not. But that doesn't mean my father isn't keeping more from us. It's not as though I can ask him outright, is it?' Which was true, of course. Any sort of question would give away the fact she'd been spending her nights spying on him. Daughter or not, I couldn't see that going down too well with the pirate. People in his position had a habit of being paranoid, and given the game we were playing it wasn't much of a stretch to imagine how two and two could quickly become a dead me.

Of course, I'd heard the name before. Who hadn't? Mara. Mistress Mara. Mara, Mistress of the Murky Depths. Mara, Lady of the Sea. But in the world I lived in she was nothing more than a myth – like Titans are myths, a wise-arsed little voice in the back of my mind heckled – a beautiful sea demon trapped forever in the confines of the long lost Water Temple. The thing is, myths are almost always based on some sort of nebulous *fact*, no matter how much time and distance from the truth distorted it over the generations. What that meant for me, for my mission, I had no flaming idea, but I figured the smart money was on believing every last thing I'd ever heard about her was true. My guess was that I had not heard a fraction of what there might be to know about her, but what I had heard was frightening enough in that *no-one-gets-out-of-here-alive* sort of way. She could drain every ounce of water from your body, leaving a dry and desiccated corpse; she could fill your lungs with water on dry land, so you drowned without any water in sight; she could make you thirst for days, so you died of dehydration, as though you'd staggered to your death in an endless desert, that dryness unquenchable no matter how much water you swallowed; she could cause the moisture in your eyes to boil, leaving you blind and screaming in those last moments; she could pollute the blood in your veins, turning it brackish; she could harden it to ice, causing it to freeze in your heart even as it tried one last time to beat; she could do all this and more. Floods, deluges, anywhere water could flow, she was the demon queen.

I felt ever so slightly sick.

'No. No. That's impossible,' Chani said, shaking her heard. She licked her parched lips. My first superstitious thought, and I hated myself for it, was that Mara's pernicious touch was already leaching the water out of the woman and in a matter of seconds I would be looking down at an empty husk, like shed snakeskin, on the ground where this stunning woman had once stood. That would be just my luck. 'She cannot have broken the seals that bind her. Believe me, it is impossible. The gates of her prison are secured by voodoo charms. Her flesh is bound by magic as old as the earth itself. Neither can be broken. It is not merely speaking a word, or shattering a chain. Breaking the seals would take years. *Millennia.* She couldn't do it from *inside* her prison. And she can't reach out through the bars, not even with her will, there are safeguards in place. There is no way for the demon to extend her malignant influence beyond the temple walls. Escape is impossible.' Despite the ferocity of her words, and her insistence, fear blazed in her eyes.

Patty looked at the voodoo woman, and said simply, 'Perhaps she has found a way.' That was Patty all over. The word impossible wasn't in her vocabulary, even when it would have been rather useful if it were.

She knew something she wasn't saying.

And I just knew it had something to do with daddy dearest.

I was really beginning to hate that man.

# CHAPTER 10

The others caught up with us.

We followed Chani through the trees, moving with more caution now, the closer we got to the Earth Temple. Finally, we could see the terracotta rooftop over the trees. There was a clearing ahead of us. I could hear noise: talking, movement. The pirates were waiting for us outside the temple.

I crept forward, so close to Chani's shoulder that I could smell her tropical scent. It was heady, natural oils, coconut, mango, papaya and so many other fruits of the rainforest. She was like a banquet for my bloody nose, which made it difficult to focus on the job at hand, namely finding Crow, stopping Crow, and, in the process, taking our first tentative steps towards saving the world. Right then there was an element of 'why me?' about it, but the truth was I enjoyed it. That was my big guilty secret. I hated sitting around on my hands. I'd much rather have been out there facing impossible odds, risking life and limb to do something *important*. That was why it was so difficult to take being discarded by the Inquisition the way I had been. There was no small part of me determined to show them the error of their ways.

'There is my father,' Chani whispered, pointing through the last line of vegetation. We were so close to the edge of the wilderness all it would have taken was one good push to shove us out into the open. I looked at the temple. It looked like any other old ruin I'd seen. It always amazed me – or should that be confounded me? – what other people chose to hold up as holy. The natives were sitting on the ground cross-legged, and seemingly oblivious to the comings and goings of Crow's pirates moving between them. None of them so much as glanced in our direction.

I counted a dozen pirates. I had O'Brian, Blake, Morris and Gruff with me, but had no idea how useful the cook would be in a scrap, or how handy the others were with a cutlass. Then there was Patty, who was worth three of any men. Along with Chani I thought the seven us would take them in an unfair fight. I held off giving the signal to charge out of the undergrowth. We had to do this just right. I could feel the nervous anticipation bubbling up in the others. I felt it too. I guess that meant I was one of them.

Of course, I wasn't an idiot all of the time. I figured Crow would have more men inside, but I'd worry about that if I wasn't dead in a few minutes.

'First things first, we have to get inside,' I said, thinking aloud. 'Crow's in there, he's up to no good, and–' Gruff looked at me like I was speaking fluent gibberish. I guess they weren't used to motivational speeches. I shrugged. 'This shit's about to get a whole lot harder if we wait around much longer.' The pirate nodded. I guess I was speaking their language after all. 'Time to bust some heads.' I added for effect. I was playing to my crowd.

O'Brian liked that.

'No,' Patty said. She didn't say it with any particular force. It wasn't loud. But the word had power all the same. I looked at her, knowing what she was going to say. It was the obvious objection. 'We should send someone back to the ship for reinforcements. We need more men.' She was right. I looked at my crew. They were a ragtag bunch at best, and while I couldn't have asked for better men beside me in a tavern brawl, I wasn't sure how useful they'd be in a real fight. But then, they weren't going up against Inquisition men, they were going up against their own kind, pirate versus pirate. That had to count for something; I just wasn't sure how much.

And to a man, of course, they would want to impress Steelbeard. There was that, too.

I knew full well the captain hadn't risked his best men. He'd sent those eager to prove themselves, like me, who were also disposable, like me. I couldn't blame him. I'm sure he hadn't expected Patty to volunteer, but short of clapping her in irons there wasn't a lot he could have done to stop her coming with me.

I shook my head.

It was always hard saying no to her, but I was getting used to it.

She'd get her own back later.

'We can't risk waiting. Who knows what they're up to in there?' I raised a hand to stop her interrupting. 'We've got to move now,' I said. 'There's no time. Going back isn't an option; it increases the risk of discovery. We'd lose any element of surprise left to us.' I turned to Chani. 'Can you get us inside? Is there another way in?'

She shook her head frantically.

'No, no, no. I cannot enter. It is forbidden. We cannot

enter the Earth Temple. It is not a Submission Day.'

I was all for observing holy rituals, especially when they were called Submission Days, even if that wasn't the sort of submission they had in mind, I'd still happily cry out 'Oh God!' for the right deity. But we didn't have the time to worry about the niceties of offending the Earth Titan if we were going to put a stop to Crow once and for all.

'Could you, though? Theoretically?'

'I have been inside before,' Chani said. 'Many times in my life. I have paid subservience to the Earth Titan, as is our way. I know the layout of the temple. But I will not set foot inside. I will not breaking the laws of my people.'

I could understand that, even if it meant we'd be going in one short, but I didn't have to like it.

'But you have to come, we need you.' It was Patty pushing the voodoo woman to help us, not me this time. I would have been slightly more whiny about it, I suspect. I mean, if I could turn my back on the Inquisition and everything I believed to take up arms with a bunch of bloody pirates to try and save the world, the least she could do was a little temple trespassing, wasn't it?

I looked at her, trying to telepathically plant all of my sacrifices into her mind so she'd get the idea, decide she was being silly and throw in her lot with us properly. And maybe I've got my own magic mojo going on, because she looked at me and said, barely audibly, 'You will have to help me… if I falter… if they try to stop me…'

I nodded once and did my best to smile reassuringly.

Behind me Gruff grunted. It was much more eloquent than anything I could have said under the circumstances.

I looked at them one at a time, trying to summon the spirit of Steelbeard even though he wasn't dead. I could have done with a little bit of his gravitas. I wanted the men to follow me into almost certain death, given the mathematics we deliberately weren't talking about. Seven on twelve was fine, but Crow's full crew probably numbered closer to a hundred, and there was a very good chance most of them were waiting inside the Earth Temple.

Thankfully, my magic mojo had run out and wasn't putting these thoughts in the men's minds.

'Follow my lead, if it looks like I need a hand, come and save me, otherwise, stay here and keep your heads down,' I said, blowing out a short sharp breath, and striding out of the trees with my hands up, as though in surrender. As far as plans went, it wasn't exactly subtle. I could only hope it would prove effective. It didn't take the pirates long to see me and realise I wasn't a native. I walked directly towards the Temple doors. They still hung open. There's a trick to doing something suicidal; if you look like you've got every right to do it, and expect it to go off without a hitch, the odds are anyone who sees you doing it will buy the illusion. At least, that was how it had always worked when I was in the service of the Inquisition.

The first of Crow's men came towards me. He had three weapons that I could see, but his best and most effective weapon against me was the three men that came two steps behind him. Four-on-one weren't the worst odds I'd faced down with a swagger. It was all about the first strike. I looked at the men as they approached. Two of them were quite possibly the missing link in the evolutionary chain, with thick skulls and thicker biceps. Getting hit by them was going to hurt. So, the trick was not getting hit. The third man was an entirely different proposition, lean, wiry, but with dead eyes. This one was going to be trouble. Unfortunately I couldn't take out the two big guys with one blow, we weren't playing dominos. The front man raised his hand and called, 'You, man, this is private property, on your way before we have to send you off, if you catch my drift?'

I didn't say anything.

Words were unnecessary. Not only that, though, I knew myself well enough to know that if I did engage with them, I'd end up saying something flippant that would incense one of them and it'd all go to hell in a handcart rather quickly from there. Better to control all the variables I could, and the one that I could most certainly control was my mouth. So I kept it zipped.

'I'm talking to you,' the pirate said, unnecessarily. There wasn't anyone else around worth his attention. It was hard not to point out the blindingly obvious, but I was going to let cold steel do the talking for me when the time came.

And the time was now.

'Boy's, teach this idiot a lesson,' he snapped.

I didn't wait for them to come at me, I stepped forward fast, driving my forehead into the first guy's face. It was elementary stuff, explosive violence and the hardest bone in my head against the softest cartilage in his. It made one hell of a mess of his nose. He went down screaming, poleaxed. Seeing stars, I snatched my sword from the scabbard on my hip, and brought it round in a sweeping arc that was just wide enough and vicious enough to disembowel the first of the two brutes, even if he was too stupid to realise his guts were unravelling beneath him. It would take a few seconds for his brain to catch up with the agony, until then he was every bit as dangerous as if I'd not just cut his jib.

The others took it as the signal to break from cover. They came streaming out of the undergrowth in eerie silence. I'd expected them to whoop and holler as they charged down the pirates, but it was utterly quiet. Not a sound. Not even a scream as Patty's dagger sprouted from the neck of the dead-eyed man. And just like that he really was dead-eyed. The only thing he was seeing was the Next World.

I dispatched the second brute with a clubbing fist to the jaw.

I almost broke my hand in the process, and he didn't so much as stagger half a step backwards. That, of course, had been my plan all along. He grinned a toothless grin at me and hit me on the side of the head so hard my brain rattled all the way back to yesterday. I wasn't so stubborn, I went sprawling across the dirt. I didn't roll so much as flop like a dead fish as I tried to get back to my feet. He came in for the kill, looming over me. And then something happened that I couldn't begin to describe with any coherence: his body twitched, his shoulders jerking back, jaw jutting forward. I thought for a moment he was dancing to someone else's tune, so to speak, but that was probably because Chani had put that idea in my head.

His shirt began to smoulder, licks of smoke curling up from it as he tried to pull it off over his head, but it was as though the cotton had fused with his skin. He couldn't get it off. And in seconds he was burning.

I turned away.

I couldn't bear to watch.

I saw Chani in the trees. She had something in her hand. It looked like a tinder stick for a musket. Smoke curled away from the brimstone tip. She blew on it and the flame caught.

Beside me, the brute burned.

Chani snuffed the flame out and he fell to the ground.

She didn't meet my stare.

She wasn't a woman to cross, that's for sure.

The others, O'Brian, Gruff, Blake and Morris went about busting heads. It wasn't graceful but it was effective. In less than a minute there were a lot of bodies lying around the clearing, a lot of broken bones, cuts and bloody smiles where mouths weren't meant to be. The natives didn't get involved, and mercifully no one came rushing out of the temple itself. It was all over before it had begun. It was ruthless and it was fast. The twelve of them had never stood a chance. But there was no denying we'd been lucky. We hadn't lost anyone, or picked up any injuries to speak of. A few cuts and bruises, that was it.

The natives watched us, but didn't move a muscle to intervene, either to aid or end the slaughter.

The old man that Chani had identified as her father was the first to stir.

I wasn't sure what to expect from him, but having just witnessed his daughter burn a man alive, I was rather hoping the apple had fallen a bloody long way away from the tree, so to speak. He regarded me curiously. For the second time in a few days I was approaching a powerful man, who almost certainly had my life in his hands, with his daughter at my side. It was becoming a bad habit.

He intercepted us before we reached the temple doors. My heart sank.

He had the power to do what twelve pirates had failed to do: stop us. He didn't need voodoo or swords, either. He only needed to look at Chani and say: 'You may not enter, daughter. It is forbidden. You know this,' in a completely calm voice. It was almost as though he were offering her a little fatherly advice, and not threatening us at all. I looked around the gathering. None of the natives carried weapons that I could see, but given the way Chani had dispatched the brute I didn't doubt for a moment that they had ways of taking care of us should the need arise. Mercifully, none of them moved to the old man's side. Not that they needed to. I was absolutely certain he could have enforced his will on Chani and the rest of us without so much as breaking a sweat. No, the natives were merely bearing witness to the warning, not enforcing it. Yet.

'I have to help them, father,' my new best friend said. I couldn't help but admire her, because there's no way on earth I'd have been saying no to the old man in her place. 'It isn't right. This isn't right. You… you are not right. You are not you. You are not the man I know. The man who raised me.' She looked at him then, stone cold hatred in her eyes. 'You are not my father. Not inside. You look like you on the outside. Your skin is your skin, your bone is your bone, but there is something else in you… And, father, if you can hear me in there, I take no pleasure in saying this, but it falls to me to do what I can to put things right. If that means helping these people, and entering the temple now, then so be it.'

I was in love.

It was going to be a short love affair, no doubt, and particularly shallow, given the impending appearance of the rest of Crow's crew and the likely backlash of any demonic force controlling her old man. I thought about trying to step in between them, but thinking was the extent of my chivalry. Chani could handle herself; there was a smouldering corpse at my feet to attest to that fact. She didn't need me fighting her battles, and, honestly, the old chieftain looked as though he was going to go into an apoplectic fit. Mix that with voodoo and anything could happen. Being in the front line was above and beyond the call of my loins. So, reluctantly, I put the mission first. At least that's my story, and I'm sticking to it.

I don't know what I'd really expected the chief to do, but instead of slapping her, or taking her in hand or doing anything to actually stop her, he simply said, 'You will regret this, daughter of the wilderness, for you are no child of mine,' and turned his back towards her. One by one the other men did the same.

I looked at Chani to see if she understood what was happening. There were tears in her beautiful brown eyes and sorrow written all over her face. When she saw me looking that changed, the sorrow replaced by defiance.

There was no time for questions. I walked past the old man, pausing only for a moment on the threshold to look back. I can't say for sure if I did it to make sure

O'Brian and the rest of the men were following, to see if Chani was with me, or Patty, or to take one last look at the outside world in case I should never see it again.

I went inside, to face Crow, his men, and whatever abominations he was in league with.

It was one of those moments when you ask yourself: *do you feel lucky?*

I felt about as lucky as a one-eyed drunk with no job, no home, no friends, no prospects and the beginnings of withdrawal making my sword arm shake.

In other words: plenty.

# CHAPTER 11

They don't make lost temples like they used to.

In my head it had all been huge vaulted ceilings and statues glorifying the Earth Titan, but instead of some huge open space, I stepped through into a rather plain antechamber. In truth it was barely a waiting room. It was more of a cave. It was dark and dank and oppressive.

But there was no sign of Crow.

I was presented with a number of unappealing alternatives, but luckily didn't have to play a game of *ip-dip* because Chani had already pushed her way through to the front. 'This way,' she said, leading us to a row of burning torches set in iron brackets on the far wall. That they were burning didn't bode well for not bumping into Crow's goons. Chani took one of the torches down from the sconce. It guttered in the breeze as she did so. 'You might want one,' she suggested, 'unless you can see in the dark?' I took the hint, as did the rest of my team. I knew we were about to enter a temple, I knew it was a holy place, I knew that spilling blood in a holy place is bad ju-ju, but I drew my borrowed sword before I took down one of the remaining torches in my left hand. Better to anger an invisible god than be skewered by a very visible pirate, after all.

Chani looked at my sword, then up at me. She didn't bother to hide her disgust. 'It's not sacred to *me*,' I said, as though that excused me of every observance. She didn't say anything, but part of me felt like I'd already brutally murdered our budding love affair. So be it. Better to have loved and lost than never to have loved at all; even if it was only for fifteen minutes. It was no great loss. I could fall in love a hundred times a day and frequently did.

The wall on which the torches had been hung created an optical illusion. I hadn't been able to see through the lie from the door: it appeared to be a single wall. But as Chani disappeared right before my very eyes, I was presented with a choice of magic, which I couldn't hope to replicate and which seemed counter-intuitive, unless the Earth Titan only wanted powerful practitioners worshipping in his temple, or trickery. I could get behind the notion of trickery. It was right up my proverbial alley these days. A cursory check revealed the slightest gap where the wall was set forward of another, creating a seamless screen that masked the real entrance to the temple. It was a simple feat of engineering, but there was a level of sophistication to it that I hadn't expected.

The real entrance to the temple lay beneath the ground.

I followed Chani as she walked down the stairs. Patty and the others followed me in single file. Without the torches we would have been blind. The stairs were treacherous, worn down by the shuffling of penitents' feet over the centuries and slick now with forest dew, or something else. *Blood?* I was good at scaring the crap out of myself at the most inappropriate times. It would have been far too easy for one of us to lose our footing on the descent. I don't know about the others, but I tried to move as silently as possible. It had nothing to do with religious observance. I just didn't want to give Crow any warning of our approach. The sound of our careful feet echoed anyway, travelling around the cold rock, with the curious acoustics of the tunnel amplifying every footstep. There was no way they wouldn't know we were coming. We sounded like a herd of elephants tramping down the stairs to me.

Chani hesitated for a moment. It was only natural. She had reached the bottom. This was the true psychological threshold for her. This was the one step that would take her irredeemably beyond, into the temple and the place of no return. I can't begin to guess how much strength even this small sacrilege took from her. I could, however, make it easier for her. 'Wait,' I rasped, pushing past her. 'I'm going in first. No arguments. This is my fight.'

I wasn't about to let her take the full brunt of the risk that opening the door entailed. It might not have been Steelbeard's way, but the notion of sending expendable bodies into the firing line first rankled. I was a warrior, above all else. If I died today that's what would be engraved on my tombstone: warrior, fighter, hero. Call it hubris. Call it macho pride. Call it whatever you want, my place was the front of the line. The glory was mine if we succeeded, the agonies were mine if we failed.

There were more brackets on the walls down here for the torches. I decided having my hands free was better than carrying a blazing torch. I could, in theory, have fought with it, if needs must, but I was much happier with having my left hand free. Besides, I was fairly sure there would be plenty of light behind the door. A torch for each of Crow's goons for a start. So I slotted mine into one of the vacant brackets.

I peered around the corner.

A moment after I'd stuck my neck out I realised that the naked flame behind me didn't worry about things like corners, and its backsplash off the damp walls stretched my shadow a long way into the temple proper. It was careless of me. The kind of carelessness that cost lives. I didn't risk pulling back abruptly. Any sudden move increased the likelihood of my shadow catching someone's attention. I resisted the temptation to curse. My mouth had gotten me in enough trouble for now. The best I could hope for was that anyone who *did* see my encroaching shadow just assumed I was one of their crew returning.

That hope died pretty damned fast when Crow called out, 'Please come in, won't you? I would hate for you to come all this way and miss the grand finale.'

I motioned for the others to stay out of sight, and then stepped around the corner.

There was no mistaking which of the men before me was Captain Crow. He wore a wide-brimmed hat at a jaunty angle, and in the band, black feathers confirmed his identity. In the flickering torchlight I could see the garland of bones he wore around his neck. It was the most macabre necklace I'd ever seen.

It was only when Chani spat 'Voodoo!' that I realised both she and Patty had followed me into the light. The sight of the bone necklace made her tremble. If it was enough to frighten her, then it was enough to frighten me.

Crow smiled maliciously. I really hate the way bad people do that. I know, I know, no one thinks they're really bad. No villain ever thinks: *mwahahahahah, I am evil, yes I am*. But there's a way these scum laugh that just sticks two fingers up to the whole notion of there being a grain of goodness in even the blackest soul. Crow could have claimed to be bullied as a child, having parents who never loved him, it didn't matter. He was the kind of bastard that tortured beloved family pets just because it made him feel good. And yes, I got all that from his nasty little smile.

'Yes indeed, my pretty little voodoo princess,' he mocked. The men at his side matched his arrogant leer. They planted their feet and stood easy, with their hands resting on the hilts of their sabres and cutlasses. I counted thirty of them. At least. Everyone's luck runs out sometime. 'Does your father know that you're down here? Oh... he does, doesn't he?' Crow mocked. 'And he's disowned you, hasn't he? Oh, what a terrible shame.

You must be heartbroken.' He inhaled sharply, and held his breath. No one moved. No one said a thing. No one made a sound until he exhaled. 'Maybe I could mend it for you? Or still it, once and for all. Which would you prefer, sweet Chani?'

'I would rather die,' Chani said, beside me.

Not the answer I would have given in her place.

'Are you sure?' He inclined his head slowly to one side until it rested on the tip of the great metal spear he carried. The move elicited a stream of curses from Chani. Patty restrained her.

'I told you that this was my fight.' I sighed. 'No one ever listens to me, do they?' I said, but no one was listening.

I don't know what I was thinking. I most certainly didn't have a plan. With thirty odd men around him I couldn't exactly walk straight up to the pirate captain and drive my sword through his guts. I walked straight up to Crow, brandishing my borrowed sword at arm's length. The tip wavered slightly – not from the DTs, I hasten to add, this was good old fashioned fear – fear that he would try and stick that bloody great spear in me.

He didn't move.

Actually, he didn't seem the slightest bit interested

in my presence. I was insulted. I mean, didn't he realise I was the hero of Faranga? I'd killed a bloody Titan! I deserved a little respect, even if he was sure in his maniacal malevolence that he was unstoppable. I'd stopped the unstoppable before.

But he only had eyes for Chani.

'Do you really think there's anything you can do here?' He shook his head. 'You're an irrelevance, girl. You and your little crew of merry men. You are bit players in my triumph. No, there's a better word for it… you are *casualties*.' He laughed then, and in one swift gesture slammed the butt of the spear into the ground. There was a long terrible moment where all I could hear was the rumbling of something deep *deep* down rising slowly towards the surface. Then the aftershocks began and the ground trembled beneath my feet.

Crow started to chant. It was some sort of incantation. I didn't understand the language, but I didn't need to. The ground shivered again, the swell of the earth becoming almost tidal as it rippled and roiled treacherously. He had to be stopped before he could complete the invocation.

His men moved protectively around him.

I spat out a curse.

For an endless moment, that long sliding second

between heartbeats and an explosion of violence, the temple was absolutely still. Then the ground began to tear open, a fissure appearing by the altar and snaking towards us. In a matter of seconds Crow and I would be on opposite sides of the divide. If that happened there'd be no stopping him.

I had no choice.

I threw myself forward instinctively, swinging my sword for his head as Chani screamed, '*Stop him!*'

One of Crow's brethren took the ferocity of my attack on his sabre, the impact shivering down my arm. I spun on my heel, changing direction to bring my borrowed blade scything around, backhanded, to cleave into his throat. For a moment the sword stuck, trapped in the bones of his neck. I had to kick him in the chest to dislodge my sword. He crumpled to the ground as arterial spray washed over us.

'Now would be a really good time for the rest of you to join in the fight!' I yelled, hacking and slashing at the next two pirates who tried to get in my way.

And all through it, Crow didn't miss so much as a syllable.

Gruff was the first to throw himself into the fray, with Patty right beside him. I caught flashes of steel in the corner of my eye as the flickering torchlight reflected off their blows. The cook leapt over the opening chasm. He had a meat cleaver in one hand, a cutlass in the other and sweat running down his face. He looked like a man possessed – right up until the moment one of Crow's henchmen's reverse sweep took out his hamstrings and left him writhing on the ground, bleeding and screaming. The goon stood over him, leering down at O'Brian as he readied the thrust to pierce his heart.

I cut the smile clean off his face, but not in time to save the cook.

There were four more men between me and Crow.

The captain was deep into his invocation now. The entire temple shook around us. The ground heaved. The walls sighed, buckling slightly, so that for one sickening moment it looked as though the Earth Temple were alive, and the walls were breathing.

Beside me, Patty went toe-to-toe with three men. She caught one wild swing on the hilt of her dagger, rolled her wrist and tore the sabre out of the man's grasp. A second later she stepped in and opened him up from balls to throat in one swift slice. She darted out again as the man tried desperately to scoop his entrails back into the gaping wound in his stomach as they slipped and slithered around his clutching hands. He was dead, he just didn't know it yet.

Chani was no less ruthless, though she didn't need any conventional weapons to engage the enemy. She said something I couldn't catch because of the sound of a deep *crack* that resonated up out of the gaping chasm and the impossibly loud *snickering* and *snacking* of claws coming from down there.

Normally this would be a moment where I'd will the ground to open up and swallow me, but given the fact the ground *was* opening up the last thing I wanted was to end up down there.

I surged towards Crow. It was what my old drillmaster had called a suicide charge. It lacked any finesse or subtlety, but what it lacked there it made up for in sheer bloody stupidity. That's what made it an effective move. Sometimes.

I ignored the bite of a sword digging into my right arm, using my weight to barrel the pirate from his feet, and was one-on-one with Crow. I wouldn't have long, I knew. If I survived it would be one of those moments I'd look back on for a long time and wonder if I could have done anything differently. I don't think I could, really.

Crow offered the shaft of the spear in defence.

I swung, putting everything I had into the blow. Patty moved in beside me, protecting my back. I could *smell* Chani close by, too.

Metal struck metal and I felt the shock chase up my arm. The impact stung my shoulder so much that I let out a yelp of pain. My hand sprung open, as though jolted by an intense pulse of energy, and I lost my grip on the sword. It started to slip out of my open hand. I leaned forward, unbalanced, trying to snatch it back before it fell.

Crow didn't care by then. I was basically helpless. He could have finished me with one blow.

He didn't.

He slammed the spear into the ground again, this time with so much force the crack tore open with one god-awful shriek. The violence of it threw me from my feet. I went sprawling, the sword spinning out of my hand, landing right on the edge of the yawning chasm that split the temple in two. An inch more and the weight of the blade would have tipped over the centre of gravity and sent my sword falling end over end into the abyss. I scrambled towards the edge on all fours and grabbed it before the next tremor hit.

Even as my hand closed around the hilt, the ground heaved again. It was like being on a storm-tossed sea.

There's just something fundamentally wrong when you can't trust the ground beneath your feet. The earth ripped. And a huge crab-like claw rose up out of the gaping chasm.

'RISE! RISE!' Crow howled, his voice a raucous triumphant caw as the thing crawled out of the subterranean pit. 'RISE UP! COME TO ME! OBEY ME!' And if that wasn't the cry of a megalomaniac nutcase, I'm not a hero, and given everything I've done, it's safe to say I am. Crow had well and truly gone off the deep end and was swimming in lunatic-infested waters. 'HEAR ME! I summon you! By the might of the Titan Harpoon, I summon you! RISE UP!' The thing hauled itself up out of the belly of the earth, claws *snickering* and *snacking* manically.

I didn't know what I was looking at.

No… I *knew* all right, I just didn't *like* what I saw.

Up out of the depths of the earth came a huge green-tinged armoured shell that dwarfed me. A mass of never-ending fibrous tree roots clung to it. The thing had a recessed turtlehead and emerged as it flexed its enormous arms. It took me a moment to realise why each ponderous movement it made was so incredibly loud. Its body was made of stone. Every movement was accompanied by the screams of stone on stone. It had multifaceted eyes, like gemstones set in its thick skull and a bloated worm-like body with what looked like lava broiling where its belly ought to have been. There were legs sprouting from its back, like some gigantic ant, with pincers on the end, constantly *clicking* and *clacking, snickering* and *snacking*. This thing was monstrous by any definition of the word.

I'd never seen it before, but I knew what it was.

Crow had released the Earth Titan, the bloody idiot.

And I was going to have to put it back in the ground.

# CHAPTER 12

The Titan heaved itself free from its earthly prison, shaking dirt free with every twist and shake, like a drowned dog. There was a chasm *and* a Titan between us! I despaired. I could have killed the idiot. I couldn't believe that Crow had freed one of the Titans. What was the idiot thinking? I looked at the weapon in his hands, sparking with raw energy: the Titan Harpoon. If it could raise the spawn of the gods, and control it, then the chances were it could destroy it, too.

Or at least I could hope it would.

Hacking at the creature with my sword wouldn't even be a distraction, I'd just be like a gnat buzzing around its face. The Titan slammed a huge clubbing fist into the ground, sending more seismic tremors rippling through the temple floor. Tiles cracked. I danced back a step and then two more, conscious of the chasm between us and the fact the Titan's reach far exceeded it.

First order of business was to stay the hell out of its clutches.

Those pincers came at me first, the hideous *clicking* and *snacking* whistling past my ear as I barely managed to throw myself out of the way. I hit the dirt hard and rolled on my shoulder, coming up with the sword straight out in front of me. I passed it from hand to hand, as though the glittering steel might hypnotise the Titan. A root snaked across the ground, trying to coil around my foot. I slammed the sword into it, cleaving clean through the tendril. The Titan bellowed its pain and rage as the root flapped away like a dying fish on the dirt. Well, at least the big guy knew he was in a fight now.

Actually, that might not have been such a good thing. Ignorance is bliss and all that.

Those oversized ant claws snatched at the air in front of me. I hurled myself out of the way again, but only just fast enough this time. The tip of one of them caught at my sleeve, tearing a rent in the cloth.

There was blood.

I didn't like the sight of blood, especially when it was my own. I wasn't squeamish; it was just a good indication the fight wasn't going to end well.

I shuffled around, trying to keep all of the Titan's extra appendages in view without taking my eyes off its huge clubbing fists.

One of them *whumped* through the air about an inch from my nose; the air displacement was enough to knock me from my feet. I looked around frantically for the others. Patty was fighting for her life. Gruff was bleeding from the head. Blake was down. So were a lot of the pirates. I caught a glimpse of the strangest sight, a pirate putting the barrel of his flintlock to his temple and pulling the trigger. A puff of gun-smoke blue came from the shadows where Chani had retreated. I didn't have time to wonder what was going on, as the Titan delivered another crushing blow and I didn't get out of the way of this one.

The huge stone fist slammed into my shoulder. I felt something break in there. The borrowed sword flew out of my hand. I went down on my knees. Another blow and my insides would have been forcing their way out to decorate the temple walls.

I tried desperately to move, but the sheer agony in my chest and shoulder from the Titan's fist was a killer. From the corner of my eye I caught sight of Patty slashing at a trailing vine with her knife. I hadn't realised that the

Titan had somehow brought the vegetation to writhing life around it – or was *part* of it. I wasn't about to worry about the little things. There was a bloody great big one to deal with. Ah, joy. Patty stepped forward and slashed her blazing torch right across the bulk of it. It wouldn't kill the Titan, but it put a crimp in its style, for sure. The vegetation writhed, a high-pitched shriek coming from the mass of roots and leaves. Chani drew her knife and did the same. Only Gruff held back, but he was bleeding so badly now he could barely see for the film of blood across his eyes.

Crow raised the harpoon in my direction. Having seen the way it tore the earth asunder there was no way I was going to stay on my knees and take it; I wasn't a tavern girl to be bought for a couple of coins an hour. I hurled myself forward; but, already on my knees, it was hard to get any real momentum or distance. I hit the ground hard, cutting my palms up on the broken stones the earthquake had ripped up as I skidded to a stop just shy of the edge. I looked up as a bolt of lightning crashed, searing the air of the temple and throwing up a shower of flint and mud and broken stones and exposing another deep rent in the earth. I didn't have time to worry about what damage the Titan Harpoon might do to something as fragile as me. Crow was already heaving the weapon back to slam it into the ground again. I wasn't sure the temple could withstand a third strike.

I had to trust Patty and Chani to keep the Earth Titan busy. Not just them, I realised, the thing was also crushing the life out of one of Crow's men. It didn't discriminate, it seemed. We were all fair game. And I had to get across the chasm. It seemed to have grown wider in the moment I was on my hands and knees, as though still stretching beneath the stress of the Titan Harpoon's aftershocks. There wasn't a second to lose. I stood up. My shoulder was sending agonised reminders to my brain. I backed up five steps, giving myself a short run up, then launched myself over the chasm.

I didn't look down.

I'd learned my lesson from the rope bridge.

Even so, I got the sickening – sinking – feeling that I wasn't going to make it. I saw the far side coming up fast, but I was losing momentum and height faster. I kicked out, wheeling my arms madly. My feet missed the edge of the chasm, slamming my shins on the edge and I was sprawling forward.

I lay on the ground looking up at a leering Crow as he prepared to spear the Titan Harpoon square in the middle of my chest. The Harpoon slammed down just as I rolled onto my damaged shoulder. I screamed in *agony*. The world went black. But the fact I could hear my own screams and wasn't dead had to be a good thing.

The ground heaved again.

Huge chunks of masonry from the ceiling began to fall. A slab of stone crashed down behind me. It caught the edge of the chasm and tumbled down. I didn't hear it hit the bottom.

I didn't have a weapon.

I didn't need one. I heaved my battered body up and stepped in fast, driving my fist into Crow's stomach. It wasn't a clean punch, but it was enough to distract Crow from disembowelling me with the harpoon, so it was without doubt the best I'd ever thrown.

I drove in a second punch, an uppercut with my left, then as he doubled up, drove my knee up into his chin, rattling a few of his teeth.

It didn't stop him.

It didn't even slow him down.

Crow came at me like a man possessed – which is exactly what he was. He swung the harpoon with all the strength he could muster. The blow cracked off my chin and sent me sprawling backwards. My hand missed the edge as I reached out to try and break my fall, and for one sickening second I felt myself falling. Luckily, Patty reached down and grabbed me by the scruff of the neck before I went tumbling down the hole.

I hadn't seen her cross the gap. I really didn't care how she had, or when. It was irrelevant. She had saved my life, it was as simple as that. I didn't thank her. I was up on my feet in a heartbeat and bearing down on Crow. This had to end.

Crow lunged forward, trying to gore me with the Titan Harpoon. I sidestepped it, but as he pulled back, unbalanced, I grasped the cold metal with both hands. He tried to shake me off. And then when he realised I wasn't letting go, he tried to drive me over the edge of the chasm.

I dug my feet in, kicking and slipping and sliding precariously over the dirt.

The chasm wasn't my only problem.

He was pushing me perilously close to the Titan.

All I could do was try and use my weight to my advantage; Crow was emaciated, as though whatever it was that had possessed him had fed off his meat until all that remained was skin and bones. I shifted my weight, even as my feet scuffed back another six inches. Crow stumbled, caught out by my sudden lack of resistance, and as he came towards me I whipped out a long leg to help him on his way.

The idiot didn't release his grip on the Harpoon, so as he started to fall, I lashed it around with more force than he could counter. His traitorous feet took him out over the edge. He hung there for a moment, staring at me, eyes blazing with manic hatred.

But the bastard refused to let go of the Titan Harpoon, and for a moment I thought he was going to take me down with him. Then gravity did its thing. It took every ounce of strength I had not to lose my grip on the harpoon. I wasn't about to let that end up at the bottom of a quite possibly bottomless pit.

Captain Crow, unlike his namesake, couldn't fly.

Crow screamed.

And kept on screaming until his cries were swallowed up by the earth.

And then it was quiet, save for the *snicker snack* of the Titan's pincers.

Patty and I stood face-to-face with the Earth Titan. We were so close to it I could see the roots and moss that festered around its mouth and eyes, and the dirt that spilled from its joints as it moved. The harpoon *vibrated* in my grasp, *thrumming* with energy desperate to be unleashed.

The giant Earth Titan lashed about left and right, with Chani and Gruff chipping away at it. It roared, opening a huge cavernous wound in its guts. The force of nature it harnessed raged, billowing out of the Titan. It drove me back away from the edge of the chasm. I couldn't stand against it. Patty didn't fare any better. The raging vortex of lava-hot wind tore at her. The heat battered her down to her knees, and bullied her back further and further towards the altar. Debris fell from the ceiling. Shadows guttered and flared, shrinking and swallowing the cavernous temple interior as the torches blazed and failed beneath the driving earth-wind.

I had one shot.

Right between the molten eyes.

Easy.

This was the kind of thing I lived for.

I heaved the Titan Harpoon back, and in that one unthinking motion sent a wave of blinding pain roaring through my shoulder, firing every nerve along the way to my brain. I slammed my front foot down, biting back a scream, and hurled the weapon straight for the creature's stone skull.

For one sickening moment I thought it was going to bounce harmlessly off it, but the point pierced the Titan's skull, and sank in to whatever lay behind the bone. Sparks of raw magic, bruise-purple in the confines of the temple, showered everyone left standing. Great arcs of lightning speared outwards, running through the cracks in the Titan's stony skin, its lava-like innards broiling and bubbling and spilling out like steaming blood to run down its hideous face.

I stood there staring at the child of the gods.

It was the second I'd killed.

Somewhere, on some karmic scale, I'd just screwed myself as far the old deities were concerned. Killing one son was unfortunate, two was downright vindictive.

And it wasn't dying cleanly or easily.

As much as I might have hoped it would shrink back into the hole it had crawled out of, it didn't, and its dying rage looked like it would bring the entire temple down on our heads.

'We've got to get out of here!' I yelled. 'The whole place is coming down!'

No one argued with me.

I could see Chani's face. I knew what she was thinking: *this is what I get for entering on a non-submission day*. I almost laughed; it was that mad *I-can't-believe-I'm-still-alive* laughter that would have left everyone in the temple in no doubt that I'd lost at least a part of my mind.

The huge centrepiece column that bore most of the weight of the entire roof started to buckle.

And the Titan wasn't done dying.

I saw my sword. It lay a dozen paces away, on the other side of the chasm. There were only a handful of pirates left standing from either side. They'd stopped trying to kill each other at least. That's one thing these guys had going for them – a sense of self-preservation. Had it been Inquisition soldiers, I'm almost certain they would have still been fighting while the temple ceiling crashed down around them, doggedly determined to win at all costs.

The pirates moved into a protective ring, and I realised it was me they were protecting. They had their sabres and their cutlasses raised, but formed a funnel for Patty and I to retreat down whilst they closed ranks around us, all enmities forgotten now that Crow was gone. I couldn't see Chani. I hoped to whatever goddess Voodoo babes prayed to that she'd already got out of there.

Several of the pirates held burning brands.

The Titan lurched, twisting and lashing out with its

huge clubbing fists as the harpoon's magic ate into its skull. It reached up, trying to grasp the end of the harpoon and wrench it out of its head, but the thing was buried deep and wasn't moving. The creature screamed in rage and pain and threw its arms wide. The stones of its chest and belly seemed to crack, fissures running through its musculature. Lava steamed in the cracks, spilling down over the Titan's body.

Fire and smoke filled the room as the pirates backed away towards the stairs.

Beside me, Patty covered her mouth with her sleeve. Roots shrivelled around us, thrashing wildly in the air.

The Titan was dying. Each second the harpoon remained lodged in its flesh increased the agony and the cries of pain, but it would not fall down. Root and branch charred and turned to ash around it. The Titan's torso seethed. And there, in the centre, as the rocks crumbled away around what by rights ought to have been its ribcage, I saw something pulsing inside: the Earth Titan's beating heart, deep inside the inferno.

The Titan's rear pincers snapped and bit at the air as it thrashed about. Somehow, one found its way through the ring of pirates and caught Patty a glancing blow across the side of the head, knocking her from her feet.

The sheer force of the blow was still enough to fling her against the wall.

Heroes do stupid things, but they do them heroically and they make a difference. That's what being a hero is all about, making a difference. It's not about doing the right thing in the face of impossible odds, any idiot can do that. It's about making a difference. And as Patty slumped down beside that wall, I made a huge leap of faith. I launched myself upwards, kicking out as I flew, and grasped the end of the harpoon even as the Earth Titan rose to its full incredible height, carrying me higher. I used all of my weight, all of my anger, all of my fear and desperation to drive the Titan Harpoon all the way in, even deeper inside its head.

The Titan roared in pain, lashing about in an attempt to dislodge me.

It was a long way down, so there was no way I was letting go of the harpoon.

Something had to give and in the end it was the harpoon that did.

Between my weight and the thing's thrashing, the harpoon tore free of the Titan's skull and I was falling.

I hit the ground *hard*.

The pain in my shoulder turned the world to black. I

was going to pass out. I knew it. And I knew that if I did I was dead. I could feel myself slipping.

The Titan loomed over me.

I could still see its molten heart beating in the middle of its cavernous chest.

This was it, last chance.

I drew my arm back and launched the Titan Harpoon with everything I'd got. The harpoon hammered home. There was a moment, a single second of pure silence, followed by a strange rushing sucking of sound, as though all of the air inside the collapsing temple was being drawn up into the Earth Titan, and then it expelled it all in a huge fireball. The flames scorched out, burning every vine and trailing root that had worked its way into the temple, battering the pirates back, charring their clothes and their skin and their hair. The heat was intense. I felt my skin begin to shrivel under it. Another huge tear opened in the ceiling, the stones screaming – and it was a proper scream, almost human in its shrill desperation as the masonry started to give – as the first great slabs of stone pulled free, falling. They hit the floor, some shattering, others cracking as fissures split through them, the impact not enough to break them apart. And then there was a real scream, and I saw that one of the pirates was trapped beneath the stones, his legs shattered. It would have been a mercy to cut his throat, but no one was in a position to be merciful, they were all too busy trying to stay alive.

The Titan was coming undone.

The harpoon sparked and spat and crackled with energy as it drained its heart.

The creature sank to its knees.

One of its insectoid feelers splintered and broke away as it hit the ground. Lava oozed out of the end, solidifying as it cooled, to form a jutting layer of fresh stone that ran down into the chasm. The claw at the end stopped *snapping*.

Another great chunk of stone came down, barely missing me. This one seemed to be holding a great many of the others in place. I looked up in horror as the vines that interlaced with the masonry and had wormed their way into every nook and cranny as though the forest was trying to reclaim the temple for its own, were ripped free and a vast section of the roof came down. The air filled with choking dust and screams. My eyes stung. I could barely see. There were outlines of light, flickering in the dust, but darkness was descending all around.

The Titan toppled forward.

As it hit the ground, the momentum of the fall drove the harpoon clean through the Titan's heart and out the other side. As the tip tore through the stone it unleashed the final huge surge of life-energy left to the gods' child. Lava bubbled and hissed and spat up out of its back, spilling down over its sides. It didn't cool quickly enough to prevent it pouring over the side of the chasm. As it solidified, the lava began to form a crusty bridge of sorts. It didn't reach the other side, but it didn't need to. It would make the jump back easier. Not that I'd be in any position to make it. I could barely move and I was losing my grip on consciousness fast. I groaned. I think. There was so much noise now and everything hurt.

I was done. Spent. Finished.

I didn't even have the strength to curl up or raise my arms to shield my head.

Debris fell all around me. It was only a matter of time before I was crushed by falling stones.

Then, with one final roar, the Titan splintered and whatever held it together gave way. The stone giant blew apart, sending rubble and rock dust everywhere. And every fragment *burned* where it fell.

Including on me.

It stung and smouldered but I didn't have the strength

to shake it off.

I lay there, thinking, hell, I'd done it: Hero two, Titans nil.

Then there was silence and I was done thinking.

# CHAPTER 13

I felt like the sky had just fallen on my head and the sky was made of solid slabs of scalding stone. In other words, I felt like a furious Earth Titan had used my body to play percussion.

I opened my eyes.

That in itself was no small miracle.

At first there was nothing.

Then there was light.

Then there was Patty.

She leaned over me, stroking my face. I was half-tempted to play dead a little while longer. Her lips were moving but I couldn't hear a word she said.

She saw I was awake.

She smiled.

That smile took the crushing weight from my bones.

I smiled back.

Normally, the first thing you'd think is: *man, it feels good to be alive.* But it didn't. It felt like crap. Everything hurt. But once the realisation that I wasn't in the Hereafter settled in, I'd no doubt start to appreciate those pains.

Slowly, my hearing started to return. I could piece together the sounds and the movement of Patty's lips.

'Where does it hurt?' Patty asked.

I pointed at my lips and puckered up. I really could be an arse sometimes. It was amazing someone hadn't tried to take me down a dark alleyway and teach me a lesson. Well, they had, but invariably they came off worse and I lived to pucker up another day.

Patty laughed.

It was *good* to see her laugh.

She helped me to my feet.

There were a handful of us left to walk out of the temple. That was better than I'd expected, to be honest.

Chani came up beside Patty. She held the Titan Harpoon in one hand like a trophy. I'd thought it was lost. I don't know how it had survived the inferno of the dying Titan's heart. There was no doubting this was the weapon I'd been sent to find. Mission accomplished. Chani brushed still smouldering embers from her hair with her free hand. She offered me the harpoon. 'It can summon Titans,' she said, 'But, more importantly, it can also destroy them.'

I took it from her, expecting the metal shaft to be hot. It wasn't. It was *icy* cold.

I tested its weight in my hand as though I'd never held it before, feeling its balance. The craftsmanship was incredible. It was a weapon fit for a hero. Holding it in my hand, I stopped missing my flintlock pistol and my rusty old sword.

I couldn't believe I had it.

Now all I had to do was get it back to the Crystal Fortress.

I almost made it sound easy.

That'll teach me to tempt the gods, having just killed *another* one of their children.

You'd think I'd know better than that, but even without opening my mouth, I had an unnerving ability to put my foot in it.

# CHAPTER 14

It was like the first breath of air I'd ever tasted. Quite honestly, I'd never been so glad to swallow a lungful of air as I was at that moment, stepping out of the ruined temple.

One of Crow's men gave me my sword back like a peace offering. I took it from him and slid it into the scabbard on my hip. It felt good to have it back. I hadn't realised how tightly I was gripping the Titan Harpoon until I saw that the blood had almost entirely left my hand. The skin was bone-white.

Of the seven I had led in there, only four of us emerged. O'Brian, Morris and Blake wouldn't be sailing with us today. I wasn't looking forward to telling Steelbeard I'd got his cook killed. I could foresee the galley in my future.

Chani pushed her hood back. Sure, I'd seen her before,

but this time I *really* saw her. Maybe it was the light. Maybe it was the adrenal climb down from the whole near death thing but I couldn't take my eyes off her. I was used to two kinds of beautiful in my world: soft, gentle, feminine beauty and harsh, strong, angular perfection. Chani was neither. She was utterly exotic.

She made to go to her father. I knew it was going to end badly before she was even halfway across the clearing towards him. The old chieftain was holding court with his tribe. He kept his back turned to her as he talked to them. I couldn't understand a word he was saying, but I didn't need to. I could tell it was some kind of lament or elegy for the Earth Titan. I guess we weren't his favourite people. Hardly surprising given that we'd desecrated his scared temple and killed the critter he'd given his life over to the worship of. I'd have been pretty pissed in his place, too.

None of the other tribesman acknowledged Chani's approach, either.

I was about one concussion away from marching right over there and banging their heads together. Patty could read my mind. She reached out and placed a restraining hand on my arm. 'This isn't our fight,' she whispered. She was right. Chani needed to do this herself, but I couldn't believe these small minded idiots couldn't see that she'd just saved their flaming village. Hell, more than that, she'd probably saved a good-sized slice of their entire world. And for that, they shunned her.

Eventually her father spoke. He still did not turn around.

'You are not welcome here, daughter. I told you what would happen if you set foot inside the temple, and yet you defied me. With one step you ceased to be a member of this tribe. All it took was to cross the threshold in defiance.' He paused for a moment. 'And all it took was one step for you to cease to be my daughter. Now go.'

Patty's grip tightened on my arm.

She knew me so well.

Chani didn't stay to be insulted. She set off for the trees. Patty ran after her, but not so quickly as to rob her of her privacy. She was thoughtful like that, Patty. It was empathy. I wasn't big on the whole empathy thing. I was more of a breaking heads kind of diplomat, and it was time for a bit of that problem-solving now.

I grabbed the chieftain by the shoulder and turned him around, not too delicately.

'I'm going to ask this once,' I said, 'And if I don't like the answer I'm going to take this harpoon I've just found and stick it where the sun doesn't shine. Do we understand each other?' The chieftain looked at me as though I was speaking in tongues. I rolled with it. It wasn't a tough question. 'Why?' I asked. 'She has just saved your life in there. . . you do know that, don't you?'

'It makes no difference.'

'Of course it does.'

He looked me in the eye. I knew his sort. Bully boys with a little bit of power. I wasn't about to let him push me about. 'What's the matter? You embarrassed because she made good on your mistake? It was you who let Crow's pirates in, wasn't it?'

'Their captain has been punished,' he said, motioning towards the harpoon. 'And so must she be. Chani has broken the law. She knew the consequences of her actions, now she must accept them.'

'But I *made* her show me the way,' I objected.

'Then she is your responsibility now,' the man said and walked away.

I hadn't saved her life; she'd saved mine, if anything. Suddenly she was my responsibility? It seemed that backwoods tribesmen could do the whole guilt trip thing every bit as effectively as an Inquisition priest. She was being made an outcast because of me. How, in all good conscience, could I abandon her?

Chani was already out of sight. I looked at the old man. I'd clenched my fist without thinking about it. It would have been so easy to flatten him, but there'd been enough fighting for one day. Instead I said, 'I killed your precious Titan. See how your precious village fares without its deity to watch over it. You'll be dead by the solstice.' As far as curses went it wasn't exactly menacing, but it wasn't exactly taking the high road, either. He ought to have been grateful it hadn't cost him any teeth.

I started after the women.

Gruff and Crow's men followed me.

It was a long way back to the ship. Or at least it *felt* like a long way.

As I crested the brow of the hill overlooking the beach, I saw that our problems were in the process of becoming a whole lot worse.

Patty and Chani were already running towards the listing ship.

This wasn't supposed to happen.

It wasn't an Inquisition ship; it was Steelbeard's. It was a pirate ship. It was supposed to be safe. I looked at the weapon in my hand. What had I done? I knew it was my fault. It always was.

# CHAPTER 15

I wasn't even halfway down the hill and I could hear the screams. I was too far away to help, but that didn't stop me running.

It was only when I caught up with her that I realised that it was Chani who was screaming. We were no more than two hundred yards from Steelbeard's ship. It was under attack. Water surged and splashed around it, the ship's hull listing in the surf as the tentacles of a great sea beast lashed at it, trying to coil, serpentine-like around the bulkhead and drag it under. I couldn't believe the Kraken had ventured this close to shore. That it was tearing a pirate ship apart left me cold. I gripped the harpoon in my hand.

More tentacles rose from the waves. They snaked across the deck, taking a hold of the Captain's cabin and tossing the ship as though it were no more than a wooden toy. Another great tentacle rose up impossibly high, its suckers slick with seaweed and the bilge of the ocean floor, and wrapped itself around the main mast. The Kraken snapped it like a twig. Sailcloth, rope and matchwood collapsed. The ship wasn't merely listing now; it threatened to capsize.

I sprinted furiously down the last part of the hill, arms and legs pumping hard, my shoulder *screaming* with every step. I was doing untold damage to the bone and tissue around it, grating the broken edges against each other, but there was nothing I could do about it. I threatened to black out with each and every step. But sheer bloody mindedness kept me on my feet. I could collapse later, right now, the fight was still going on.

By the time I had reached the harbour it was already too late.

The forces pulling on the ship's hull were irresistible. It snapped in half with shrieks of splintering wood, and began to sink from its centre as the Kraken lifted each end of the great ship from the water. One oil-slick tentacle beckoned me toward the sinking ship, and I realised in absolute horror that one of the pirates was caught in its grip.

The tentacle slithered away beneath the waves, taking the pirate down to the depths. Another tentacle lashed back and forth, and hurled a screaming pirate towards the shore. The impact broke him. The beach was like a warzone by the time I reached it, with casualties lying bent and bloody and broken on the sand. Shocked and injured men struggled to find their feet. Some couldn't stand. More splashed and staggered and fell in the water, trying desperately to try and swim ashore. They had to fight their way through the bodies of their comrades floating on the tidal swell. I saw men hanging from parts of the wreckage, trapped in the ropes and the tattered sails. Others clung to bits of broken wood as though they might guide them to safety. And then thank, well thank every god, devil, demon, demi-god, semi-god, mini-god, god-like thing, entity, imp and familiar spirit, the Kraken began retreating to the deep.

With Patty and Gruff beside me, I pushed the landing boat back into the water. I lay the harpoon inside, and jumped in. Gruff took the oars from me. 'Not with your shoulder, man,' he growled. He had a point. I let him guide us out into deeper water.

Patty leaned in close to me, her lips less than an inch from my ear. Her breath prickled my skin as she urgently whispered, 'Find him, please. Find him.' She didn't say another word all the way to the wreckage. Gruff pulled at the oars for all he was worth.

We found MacLaine hanging onto a barrel. Rum really was a lifesaver, I thought, reaching out to drag the man aboard. He was barely conscious and bleeding. I found the cut on the side of his head. It wasn't deep, but head wounds were always tricky. They could look quite innocuous on the surface, hiding all sorts of damage beneath. I washed the blood away. It just came back. I laid him in the middle of the boat.

And then my heart nearly leapt out of my mouth as Patty shrieked, '*Father!*'

She pushed herself up, struggling to stand. The sudden movement rocked the landing boat alarmingly, threatening to topple us.

"Sit down, girl!' Gruff barked. I reached out a hand to hold her before she went and did something particularly Patty-like. Gruff worked the oars hard, manoeuvring the boat in the direction she claimed to have seen Steelbeard. He grunted with every dip and pull of the oars, tiring fast. It wasn't surprising, he'd taken a battering in the temple too, but the pirate was made of stern stuff. He just gritted his teeth and pulled on the oars again and again.

I saw Steelbeard's red coat rippling out on the surface of the water.

The old Captain was face down in the water.

My grip closed on Patty's arm.

His hair looked like sea snakes feasting on his head with the way the swell made the beads and dreads writhe.

I was ready for the worst, but Patty wasn't. She pulled away from me, and, with her front foot on the side of the boat, launched herself into the sea. She swam to her father's side, turning him over in the water, and with her arm wrapped around his huge barrel of a chest, kicked and swan back to the safety of the small boat.

Safety was a relative term, given the proximity of the Kraken's tentacles.

MacLaine and Gruff helped me haul Steelbeard aboard. It was a miracle, but he was alive. Barely. The stubborn old bastard just refused to die, no matter how much of the sea he swallowed or how badly battered his body was.

I helped Patty back into the boat. It was getting crowded in there now. The men had laid Steelbeard in the middle of the decking. He looked bad. Deathly pale. He tried to say something but Patty urged him to stay quiet and conserve his strength. She knew as well as I did that there was no hope for the old man. His ribs had been crushed and there was a wet rasp to his breathing that suggested a punctured lung. Each shallow intake of breath he took was clearly agony.

He reached up and grabbed my wrist.

'Save my men,' he implored. In those three words I saw for the first time the nobility and greatness of the man. Even as he lay dying his only thoughts were for those who had put their trust in him. 'Do not...' he coughed, and the pain of that simple cough was terrifying to behold. 'Let them fall into the hands of the Inquisition...' The fire in his eyes was burning out, fast. 'Find them a new ship if you can... I beg you... Do not let them be hung like animals. If you love my daughter, do that for her. Please.'

'I'll do everything I can,' I said, and I meant it. I meant it more than I'd meant anything I'd ever said to the man before. Right up until this moment it had all been about winning his trust, using him. Now it was about being a man. I wouldn't fail him. I didn't make promises cheaply when they were being given to a dying man.

'MacLaine?' Steelbeard asked, seeing the helmsman in the boat with us.

'He'll have a sore head, but he'll be fine,' I said, looking at the helmsman. I wasn't qualified to make any such prognosis, but his injuries didn't *seem* life threatening.

The knowledge seemed to give the captain some comfort at least.

'I need…' he broke off, coughing again. When he finally gathered himself, he was a shadow of the man he had been even a moment before. The end was close, even Patty could see that. She was crying beside me. No sobs. Silent tears. It was heart-breaking. 'I need you to know…' he managed. I could barely make out his words for the constant splashing of the sea around us. I risked a look up towards the ship, though in truth there was little more than the main mast and the crow's nest above the water. There was no sign of the damned Kraken. Steelbeard looked at Patty, she seemed about to say something but he silenced her with a single finger to her lips. 'I know,' he said. And smiled. It was a father's smile. My respect for the man grew by the minute. 'I have carried a secret with me for a long time, sweet child. It is time that someone else shared my burden. And while I never meant it to be you, I only have so many breaths left in my body to share it, so you will listen, girl. And you, pirate.'

He smiled at me, and I knew I'd won his trust. What a damned hollow victory it was though. I did my best to smile back down at him.

'You already have one part of the puzzle, whether you realise it or not, though I doubt you understand what that thing is capable of doing.'

That thing. He was talking about the Titan Harpoon. I wanted to tell him that I already knew what it could do, that he could save his last words for important stuff, things he needed his daughter to know, but he was acting like a man with a burden he needed to lift, so I said nothing.

# CHAPTER 16

'I don't have the strength to repeat this,' he said, 'so listen carefully, and don't interrupt me. It will only make it harder. I need to tell you this my own way. I need you to understand the curse you have taken on, man, and I need to say sorry to my girl, but none of that is worth a damn if you don't *understand*.'

I nodded.

Patty looked as though she might object, but the look he gave her took care of that. She was still daddy's little girl, and I wasn't going to fight with him for the last few minutes of his life.

'I'll be honest, the days are so long gone, I've forgotten what it was like… but back then there were four of us… true pirate captains… We controlled everything. And I mean everything. We had a pact. We did not cross each other. We did not plunder in each other's waters. But it wasn't just avoidance, we shared information if we believed it would help one of our brethren. They were the halcyon days of piracy, believe me. The Inquisition was right to fear us.' Steelbeard broke off, laughing. That laugh quickly became a wet hacking cough. 'We were mighty. But sands shift beneath the tide. It began to crumble apart when we found ourselves in a place that was not on any charts.' he let that hang in the air for a moment, before making sure we understood exactly what he meant. 'It was a place that had been hidden from humans for a thousand years... I curse the day that I found it.'

I had a thousand questions already, but I'd promised to just let him talk. It was hard, but I knew that I stood a better chance of getting answers this way. This time when he picked his story up, it sounded more like a fairy tale than a confession.

'The four of us each reached the same place within a day of each other. It was as though we had been drawn there, the winds coming together to blow us each in the same direction... There was something wrong about the place. I can't explain it. You just have to *experience* it for yourself. It's like nowhere else in the world. And because of that none of us could go ashore at first. When the second ship arrived and then the third we knew we were being gathered, and we knew that we couldn't set foot ashore before all four of us could stand side by side. We had found the Water Temple. The place was the stuff of legend. Real legend. Not just make-believe. But even so, it had been lost for so long, even those of us who lived our lives on the water had stopped believing it was there to be found.'

'Father…' Patty began, but Steelbeard ignored her.

'The four of us went into the temple together, side-by-side. It was the last time we did anything together. I don't know what we were thinking. Perhaps we imagined we would find some long lost treasure? Some of it I remember like it was yesterday… Deep within the temple we found four seals set into a wall… They were golden plates, beyond value, things of incredible beauty. I hadn't seen their like before, so of course I had to have them. Greed. Avarice. So often the good and the bad man's downfall. We set about removing the seals. There were four of us, so it only seemed right we divide the spoils equally, one for each of us. We were still friends at that point. How were we supposed to know that our actions would free the demon, Mara?'

He didn't want an answer from me.

'She had been held prisoner there for a thousand years. A thousand years! And we undid it all in a few greed-filled minutes! She used us. She fed on our insatiable hungers, promised riches beyond imagining. And we… believed her just long enough to damn ourselves.'

He paused for a moment, gathering himself, and I was sure that was it, his last breath, but I underestimated the man. He was determined to cleanse his soul. I knew the story was the only thing keeping him alive. Soon enough he'd be at peace. For these last few minutes it was all about the story.

'She was hideous. . . but that's not right. . . she was *beautiful*, too. Terrifying. . . but enchanting. . . She could not be ignored. She stood before us. . . It was the end and the beginning of everything. Mara gave us each a token to show her gratitude. . . but there was no trust between us anymore. She placed a curse on us, binding the four of us to her service evermore. Each of us. . . we had to find something for her. . . And were denied rest until we did. There would be no death. No peace. Not until we had completed the tasks she bound to us.' Steelbeard reached out slowly, his hand finally closing on the Titan Harpoon. 'This was given to Crow, Slayne was given the Sacrificial

Knife, Garcia had the magical Bone Hand and I was given this.' Steelbeard reached inside his shirt and pulled out a small golden disc that hung on a chain around his neck. 'This is the Amulet of the Earth. I am sure that this is why we were able to escape her clutches... though I'd rather believe it was because I loved something more than gold or riches.'

He let go of the harpoon and took his daughter's hand. The inference was obvious. They both had the beginnings of tears glistening in their eyes, but neither of them was about to cry. They were too stubborn for that. It was a family thing. Oxen, the pair of them. The pain was receding. It would be over soon enough. But not until Steelbeard finished his confession. His lips were dry and cracked. I wished I had water to share with him.

'This damned amulet had been hidden for so long, but once I suspected that you were trying to prove yourself to me, I couldn't be sure you wouldn't stumble across my hoard, so I removed it. I haven't worn it for so long... it is a heavy burden to bear... I was so frightened you would stumble upon it without knowing what it was...' he squeezed Patty's hand. 'You have never needed to prove yourself to me, girl.' He smiled at Patty. She was finding it harder and harder to hold back the tears. She didn't want them to be the last thing he saw. That wasn't an image to take to the Hereafter.

He turned his gaze my way.

'You have to recover the other artefacts,' he said. He made it sound so simple. I smiled softly. I knew the 'simple' things were always the most difficult to achieve. Always. 'When you have them… take them to the Water Temple… all of them… swear it… swear you will take them back.'

I nodded.

'No… swear it.'

I laid my hand on his chest. 'I swear.'

'Together they are capable of destroying Mara once and for all,' he said. 'You must succeed. For all of us.'

His last words would haunt me, night after night, never leaving me alone in the dark, until I came good on my promise. That's why you never swear an oath to a dying man. It's always going to come back and bite you on the arse.

Steelbeard took one last breath, a little deeper than before. I could feel his pain.

He closed his eyes and I knew that it was over.

Patty leaned forward, resting her head on the dead man's chest.

It was only later, when I was trying to work out how I could possibly come good on my promise that I realised Steelbeard hadn't told me where to find the legendary Water Temple.

Well, why would he want to make it easy for me?

# CHAPTER 17

'Seize them! Arrest them all!' Moments after the cry came, armed men rushed out of hiding, storming the beach. In a matter of minutes things had gone from bloody awful, to heart-breaking, to desperate, to much, *much* worse.

It really wasn't my day, despite the fact that I had slain a Titan and won the trust of one of the world's most infamous pirate captains. For anyone else that would be a *good* day. I wasn't most people. For a start, I was cursed.

The pirates who had managed to drag themselves ashore were not exactly in a position to resist as the Inquisition forces took up positions, muskets primed. I knew so many of the men, if not by name, by face at least. There was no way we could fight them all. And there was no doubting that they were ready to fill anyone who tried full of lead shot.

Steelbeard's men stood with the few that remained of Crow's. The pirates offered no resistance. Chani stood in the middle of them, looking utterly out of place. She had pulled her hood up as though it would make her invisible. I reached out to take Patty's hand, but she pulled away. It was a tiny gesture, but it stung. Just a little bit. I knew she was hurting. I only wanted to protect her because I recognised the man barking orders on the beach: Commandant Sebastiano.

Inquisition men dragged our landing boat up the shallow slope of sand.

Sebastiano was waiting for us to disembark.

'More lives than a bloody cat,' he said, seeing me help MacLaine out of the boat. 'But maybe that was number eight you just used up, eh?'

I didn't bother arguing, and Sebastiano wasn't listening. He only had eyes for the harpoon.

'So this is what all the trouble has been about?' He reached into the boat for the prize. It was so like him to try and steal the thunder and the glory. He was that kind of officious little prick whose face was due a collision with something hard and fist-shaped. I would have loved to oblige. It would no doubt have ingratiated me even further with my new comrades, but sometimes discretion was the better part of punching the sycophant's lights out, or at least I tried to tell myself that.

'What are you doing here?' No one had mentioned any back-up being sent, or, more specifically, that Sebastiano would be following. They must have set out a day after us, no more than that, possibly even less, and anchored their ship off another part of the island. I worked through the alternatives, coming over land while we had made our assault on the Temple was a typically Sebastiano thing to do. They lured the Kraken here, I realised sickly. Steelbeard's death *was* all my fault. I felt sick.

'Did you think you were *trusted*? You? A drunken sot? Her? The daughter of a damned pirate? Oh, yes of course you were trusted, about as far as Carlos could throw you. You're through. And she,' he motioned towards Patty, who was resolutely refusing to leave her dead father to Sebastiano's men. 'Will be joining the rest of the crew as they face trial. That, my friend, is what we call a happy ending.'

I wanted to tell him what the girls in Booze's employ called a happy ending, but bit my tongue. Of course, they did that, too, but it cost a little bit more.

In the distance I heard the not so delicate sound of

cannon fire. A smile of satisfaction flickered across Sebastiano's face. I wasn't ever going to think of him as 'Commandant', that, at least, was one perk of having been booted out of the Inquisition. I didn't have to bow and scrape to the likes of him. 'It would seem that today is my lucky day. Two pirate crews brought to justice? I wonder how they'll honour me? A statue perhaps?' Sebastiano sneered. I was thinking more 'early grave', there was a headstone involved, after all, and that was almost a statue. 'I gave the order to scuttle Steelbeard's ship. There's only one way off the island, now, and that's with me.' I half-expected a maniacal laugh. 'And those who choose to sail with me will disembark at the Crystal Fortress, and not a moment sooner. Though there is the promise of a nice little view from Gallows Point to encourage them. Those that survive the journey back, of course.'

Pirates were never given a trial; that was a fact of life, just like the birds and the bees. They were bought before the Inquisition, had charges read out and sentences passed. There wouldn't be any opportunity for the men to plead. The word innocent would never be heard within a hundred miles of them. These men already had an appointment with the hangman. So, in the matter of minutes since I'd promised a dying man I'd protect his crew and save them from the rope, I'd managed to wade ashore in time to see them arrested by the very people I'd promised to protect them from. This whole promise-keeping thing was going to be a real pain in the arse. Sure, the pirates knew the score. They signed up for it when they took Steelbeard's coin, but not Patty. She was Steelbeard's flesh and blood, but she wasn't part of that life. And I was damned if I was going to let Sebastiano string her up.

I felt my fist clenching as I asked, 'Am I under arrest?'

Sebastiano laughed. There was no joy in the sound. It was a bitter miserable laugh, like the man himself. 'Why would you be? Your mission was clear, wasn't it? Find the weapon, put it into Inquisition hands. You have found the weapon, and mine are the hands of the Inquisition. My only instruction is to return you to the Crystal Fortress. No doubt the Commandant wishes to see you properly rewarded. After all, thanks to you, we have two less pirates on the seas, and a weapon that will destroy the Kraken,' he said, lifting the harpoon in a show of victory. 'You're a damned hero.'

I was damned, that much was right.

His words weren't exactly greeted with joy by the pirates. If they hadn't been restrained things could have turned very ugly. They weren't exactly pretty as it was.

'It's a mistake,' I said. What I was thinking was, in his hands it'd most likely end up at the bottom of the sea.

'I have my orders,' he said, already turning his back on me. He had absolutely no interest in anything I had to say. 'You are, of course, welcome to travel in the hold with the rest of the scum, if you wish. I won't stop you.'

Sometimes life is about which battles to fight, and picking the right ones. It was a long enough voyage that the situation could change – or more accurately could be made to change. I just had to bide my time. The day wasn't won or lost just yet. Besides, I was finding it increasingly difficult to focus through the pain in my shoulder. 'Patty helped us locate her father. She was integral in my locating the harpoon. It isn't right that she be treated like a common pirate.'

'And yet that is exactly what she is. And believe me, in all the things that were said, all the promises that were made to that young lady, immunity was not one of them. My instructions are to arrest every last one of them, her included. My only regret is that I cannot clap that bastard Steelbeard in irons.'

'There is a woman,' I said.

'Isn't there always?' Sebastiano leered.

'A native. Painted face. Pretty. Her name is Chani. She will be coming with me.'

'Will she now?'

'Yes,' I said, my tone brooking no argument.

Sebastiano barely shrugged. He couldn't care less. She wasn't an enemy of the Inquisition. And because of that, she didn't matter. When I set out my mission might have been to locate and obtain a weapon with which we could take down the Kraken, but things had changed. There was a bigger enemy than the Kraken – and more stubborn promises than the one I'd made to Commandant Carlos. I owed Patty. I was in debt to her father…

But I was still part of the Inquisition, wasn't I?

It might not have felt much like it, but I was as bound by orders as Sebastiano, and if the Inquisition had recalled me to the Crystal Fortress to face my fate, then so be it.

I rubbed a hand across my jaw. The stubble was more beard than five o'clock shadow now.

I needed a drink.

Badly.

Sometimes the answers really did lie at the bottom of a bottle.

'Are we done?' I asked.

'Yes.'

'Good. One question: do you have a healer on board?'

'Naturally.'

'Good.'

It was only then, as I moved my collar aside and Sebastiano saw the bone jutting out beneath the skin, that I allowed myself to collapse into his arms.

He sidestepped me, and I hit the sand.

# CHAPTER 18

Chani did something to relieve the pain in my shoulder. I don't know what she did. I didn't ask, and I didn't want to know. I slept on deck, if you could really call it sleep. It was fitful and I barely got close to actual rest. Although Sebastiano made no complaints about Chani travelling on board he did make a big deal out of the fact that there was only one cabin available for me and my 'guest'. He was not concerned about propriety or practicality, he just wanted to make it as difficult as possible on principal, but sleeping arrangements were the least of my worries. My life was complicated enough. So, for the first time in forever, I did the chivalrous thing and let her have the room, despite her protestations. I only needed the spare blanket. I thought about sleeping in one of the Jolly boats, but the planking that formed the bench seats made sleeping impossible.

Instead I huddled up in a sheltered corner and settled down for the night.

My shoulder was still numb, but it had stopped sending out shooting pains and the bone didn't jut out against the skin anymore. Chani had worked some kind of healing on me. No doubt that tainted me even more in the eyes of the Inquisition. I'd got native healing in my blood. Well, screw them. It was nice not to be in agony for a while.

I started to drift.

Sebastiano's plan, as best I could discern, was to deliver the pirates to the nearest Inquisition fortress before making the onward journey with the spear. I assumed he'd not taken on sufficient supplies to feed all of the prisoners and wanted to be rid of them as soon as possible – one way or another. As far as my immediate future was concerned, the only question was: what was I going to do next? I couldn't exactly stand by and watch Patty sent to her death, and a one-man mutiny wasn't going to get far. I know it was irrational, and probably grief-driven, but in my conscience I'd made both her and Steelbeard's crew my responsibility. That's what comes of making deathbed promises to a man like him. It didn't matter that we'd only known each other for a matter of days, I had promises to keep and that meant I had choices to make.

'I thought I might find you here,' Chani said, drawing me from my thoughts. She hunkered down beside me. To an outsider it might have looked as though I was asleep. The illusion didn't stand up to close scrutiny.

'You thought right,' I said.

'Do you want to talk about it?'

'It?'

'Whatever it is that is bothering you?'

I said nothing.

'Is it something you need to sort out for yourself? A man thing? Pride?'

I smiled. She was uncomfortably good. 'There's nothing to talk about. Promise.'

'Really? If that were true wouldn't you be sleeping in a nice soft bed rather than huddling up on the cold deck? It's not like you would have to sleep *with* me. I would be more than happy to take the floor.' I looked at her dark earnest eyes. She wasn't smiling. There was no joking now. No teasing. 'I owe you everything.'

'You don't,' I said, sort of shuffling and trying to sit up. 'Believe me. I, on the other hand, owe you.' I touched my shoulder. 'And in more ways than just this. If I hadn't forced you to help, you would still be at home with your family, your people, instead of being cast out.'

'That doesn't make me your responsibility.'

'It does,' I said, and I meant it.

'It is not that simple, is it?'

'It rarely is, but for once I don't know what you are talking about.' I smiled wryly.

'Then let me be a little more blunt. I am not blind. Patty. You care about her. If you didn't you would not be sleeping out here in the cold, would you?'

I said nothing. There was nothing to say.

'Ah,' Chani said. 'You see her as your responsibility too?'

'She's no one's responsibility,' I said. But there wasn't a lot of strength behind my protest. If she'd been here instead of locked up in the brig Patty would have slapped me for lacking faith in my convictions, no doubt.

'Really? I may not have known you long, but that's not how it looks to me. You, my new friend, are a hero only too willing to take the weight and woes of the whole world on your shoulders.' I couldn't argue with that assessment of my flawed psyche. I scratched at my eye socket. Sometimes I missed being able to see the world with two eyes. Other times I was grateful that the eye patch gave me something to hide my thoughts behind. 'I can read your soul,' she said, and I didn't doubt her for a moment. Chani had a gift. I remembered that flash of blue as the pirate blew his own brains out, and the mirrored spark of voodoo coming from the shadows where she hid. She had power. But that wasn't why I listened to her. I listened because even an idiot like me could tell she was right. 'If you care for her, which you do, if you feel responsibility for her father's men, which you do, then believe me, you cannot abandon them to their fate. It would haunt you for the rest of your life.'

'Lots of things haunt me,' I said, but she was right. Here was this woman who barely knew me, and she had reached the same conclusion as I had, but put it in such simple terms I really couldn't ignore it. There was a reason I couldn't sleep. If I was going to help them it meant turning my back on the Inquisition, turning my back on *everything* my life had stood for, everything that had ever made sense to me. It meant, in effect, turning my back on my life.

But if the choice was between staying with the Inquisition or saving Patty then it was no choice at all.

'I may need your help,' I said.

'There is no *may* about it. One man cannot wage war against so many enemies.' It was hard to think of them as my enemies. They had been a family to me for so long. But she was right. I'd crossed a threshold in my mind, if not in deed. I had to start thinking of them as my enemies. 'It is time that I shared with you some small secrets of voodoo,' she said. 'You will need them. But,' she glanced over her shoulder, checking for prying eyes, 'we should find somewhere more private. Come into the cabin with me. I promise I shall not take advantage of you.'

# CHAPTER 19

We didn't sleep a wink that night, or the next. But I didn't feel exhausted. I felt invigorated. Chani was a patient teacher, and after my initial resistance to the notion, I was an apt pupil. Regardless, I hoped I'd never have to use the tricks she taught me.

By the time the third morning came we were at anchor and preparations were being made to have the prisoners taken ashore.

Once they were inside the fortress it would be *much* harder for us to liberate them.

I had come to a few difficult rationalisations during the preceding days, but the biggest one was that I was prepared to sacrifice Crow's men to get the job done. And if it cost the lives of the men sailing under the Inquisition flag, so be it. Obviously I would have preferred a bloodless revolution, but beggars couldn't be choosers.

Chani had made me repeat the gestures and the incantations over and over again until I had perfected them. She was insistent, even the slightest slip, a single misplaced syllable could be disastrous. I knew the gestures, down to the subtlest twitch of the fingers, and the order in which to throw certain compounds into a fire should I need to conjure up an illusion. And although I knew that this was barely the tip of her knowledge, I had something in my armoury beyond shot or sword. The Inquisition would not expect that. And I was going to need to drive home that surprise, and then some, if I was going to walk away from this.

I wasn't made for the sailor's life.

It took Sebastiano less than an hour to work out that taking advantage of my seasickness was a great way to add additional torment to our time together. It also meant that when I asked to go ashore while the pirates were transferred, he didn't make a big thing out of it and I got a place on one of the landing boats. Sebastiano himself was the first to be taken ashore. It was all part of his power play; he wanted to be seen arranging for the prisoners to be turned over to the governor of the fortress. All that was left was the paperwork and protocol, two things the officious little dick was well versed in. It meant that we wouldn't have a lot of time to work Chani's tricks, but I only needed a minute.

Two men rowed us ashore.

Sebastiano clambered out of the boat. There was a lackey waiting to help him onto the landing stage. He marched away without another word, which suited me just fine. Everything he had to say had been said while we were on board ship. He expected his orders to be followed religiously. The pair who had rowed the boat to the jetty waited patiently for Chani and I to disembark, but we had other plans. As soon as Sebastiano had moved out of earshot Chani had begun sub-vocalising some very precise words, words that *demanded* the attention of the boatmen. It was one of the techniques she'd tried to teach me, but because of our makeshift classroom it had been impossible for me to test my aptitude, so it was better that Chani enchanted the pair. And she did. Hell, they were Inquisition men, they probably hadn't seen a halfway decent woman in months so she wouldn't have needed voodoo to wrap them around her little finger, but it was good to be on the safe side. A few well-chosen words whispered in their ears and she had the two men in her thrall, and like lovesick puppies they would do whatever she asked.

I climbed up onto the jetty and held out a hand to help Chani but she ignored it. She extricated herself from the boat gracefully without my help. Side-by-side, we watched as the two men rowed the boat back towards the ship. We had a few minutes before they returned. If Chani had been successful with her pirate-whispering, then the first men to come ashore would be part of the crew; the armed men who had arrested everyone on the shore. They would arrive ahead of the pirates to ensure that no one would escape. The oarsmen would have conveyed this revised order with all of the earnest sincerity they would have if it had come from Sebastiano's own lips.

While we waited, Chani gathered together kindling and started a small fire on the planks of the jetty. She'd explained it to me; the elements of the earth that she carried in a pouch would enhance the voodoo, meaning she could enchant more men.

'What's going on here?' the leader of the guards asked, seeing us as he came ashore in the boat. The rest of the Inquisition men quickly climbed out of the boat and, with a nod, sent it back for the first consignment of prisoners.

I put myself in between Chani and the men as she

began her incantation. She sprinkled dust into the flames, sending red smoke into the air. I joined her in the chant this time, adding my voice to hers, and my strength. I had no idea what the words meant, but I knew how each syllable sounded, and as far as the voodoo itself was concerned that was all that mattered. I did not hesitate. I dropped a handful of the powder she had given me into the flames and tried not to choke as the sudden stench threatened to overpower me.

I heard the sound of weapons being drawn. It didn't make a difference. I carried on chanting. If this did not work we'd be dead before the pirates swung from the rope.

Chani whispered a single word and as one the men let out a cry and dropped their swords as though stung by them.

'What do you men think you are doing? Pick them up! At once!' Chani barked out the command, but the voice… it wasn't hers. It was Sebastiano's.

The men obeyed without hesitation and stood to attention ready to receive their orders.

I was beginning to understand just how dangerous this woman really was.

The fire had almost burned out when the boat returned with the first of the prisoners. As I'd hoped, they were all members of Crow's crew. I didn't owe them anything. But that didn't mean I couldn't give them a fighting chance. Manacles made it harder for them to clamber ashore but once they were lined up Chani gave the order for them to be released.

'Go,' I said. 'Run. Before Sebastiano returns. You have a chance at life. That's the best I can do for you.' They didn't need telling twice. They ran as though their lives depended on it, which they did. I only hoped they'd prove to be a diversion for our own escape.

Chani reminded the boatmen that Crow's men were to be brought ashore before any of Steelbeard's and the boat set off again. Not that a lot of them remained after the massacre at the temple.

'How long will the spell hold?'

'I have no idea. I have never tried to control so many at one time. It may last for days or I may lose my grip on their souls within minutes.'

The second group of pirates couldn't believe their luck as their shackles were released and the chains unthreaded. I was surprised that the boat was not full. I'd expected them to crowd in to the point of sinking once they'd seen their companions take heel and run for the hills. 'Is this all of you?'

The boatmen didn't respond. They couldn't see or hear me, I realised. One of the pirates nodded as the guards freed them from their chains. 'Some of the men tried to escape. The Inquisition shows no mercy.' What he meant was Sebastiano had executed any man he thought might be trouble.

I caught myself on the brink of apologising on behalf of the Inquisition, but I wasn't one of them anymore, and anything I said on their behalf would have been putting words into their mouth that they would never have dreamed of saying. The Inquisition apologised to no one. 'Go,' I said instead. 'Run to the hills. Don't look back.'

Chani and I returned to the ship with the guards.

She whispered more instructions to him on the short journey, her voice becoming a constant susurrus barely audible over the waves. She didn't pause for a single breath, repeating the words over and over again, the orders word perfect every time. Without doubt this was the most dangerous part of the plan. This was where it could all go tits up. If I were still a religious man I would have offered a quick prayer. I'm not, so I didn't. But if a bored deity happened to be looking our way I wouldn't have complained if they wanted to lend a helping hand.

We let the guards climb into the ship ahead of us,

leaving the two boatmen ready and waiting to take more men ashore. The one Chani had primed was already barking orders by the time we were both on deck.

'There are traitors on the island, the fortress is riddled with enemies of the Inquisition! I need you ashore! Now! The prisoners have escaped! They have taken Commandant Sebastiano!' It was a virtuoso performance, simple and compelling.

These were Inquisition men. They were used to following orders blindly. Theirs was not to reason why. The man spoke with such conviction it was as though Sebastiano himself gave the orders.

The boat filled quickly. The oarsmen set out for the jetty. Every man in the landing boat was fired up, ready to fight. The rest didn't wait for the boat to return, they lowered the second landing boat and crowded into it. There were six men who couldn't find a berth. We watched them from the guard rail, hardly able to believe our luck and their stupidity as they left us alone. I scanned the hills. I couldn't see any of Crow's men. I had given them time, what they did with it was down to them.

I looked at the six stragglers. They were beginning to understand the severity of their situation as Patty led more than fifty men onto the deck. None of the pirates looked particularly happy, but then three days in captivity will do that to a man. They shielded their eyes from the harsh sun as they stumbled into the light. 'You've got a choice,' I said. 'Sail with us, or swim ashore. No one is going to harm you.'

They all decided to swim ashore.

I saw a familiar face among the crowd.

'Looks like we've got us a new ship, Mister MacLaine,' I said, feeling rather happy with myself. Promises kept: one. 'But I'm going to need your help if we're going to get this thing out of here.'

The helmsman looked at me as though I'd lost my mind, then seemed to realise there were six Inquisition men doing a frantic crawl back to the distant jetty, and no sign of any of them aboard. He looked at me again, with newfound respect. 'Where to, Cap'n?'

'Anywhere away from here, Mister MacLaine. That'll do for starters.'

He laughed, and started barking out orders. In under a minute we had wind in our sails.

I could see an enraged Sebastiano on the jetty.

He did not look happy, which conversely made me quite happy.

I had no idea of how long we would have before they

sent someone in search of us, or if we'd enjoy protection from the Kraken, as technically we were on an Inquisition ship. But we had a head start.

'Best place for a pirate to lie low is amongst other pirates,' MacLaine said, standing beside me at the wheel. We'd been sailing for hours. I still didn't particularly like it. I'd never get my sea legs. 'There's only one place for that.' I waited for him to issue the order. An easy smile spread across his face. 'We sail for Antigua!'

'That we do, Mister MacLaine. That we do.'

My decision had been made for me.

I was a pirate now – a real one, all ties to the Inquisition severed. No turning back. No retreat. No surrender.

Bollocks.

# CHAPTER 20

Antigua. The very name sent shivers down the rigging of my spine. The place was a den of thieves, a haven for villains and every form of scum known to man. It was a pirate's kind of place. In other words, a place the Inquisition didn't dare to set foot. It was perfect for our needs. I knew what the Inquisition knew, I knew how they thought, and we could use that to our advantage. Launching an attack on Antigua would serve one purpose – it would unite the pirates, and right now the Inquisition was in no position to go up against their combined might. No, there were advantages to leaving a place like Antigua well alone, especially when warring pirate captains meant splintered factions amid their ranks, which meant no alliances, or uneasy ones. Raiding ships sailed alone and the Inquisition could – in theory at least – pick them off one by one. Of course, it was never that simple. When one ship went down another would set sail. But given the decimation of their fleet, war on the pirates wasn't the priority it had once been.

All that mattered to us was that Antigua offered sanctuary for any pirate ship.

Gruff emerged from below decks triumphantly waving a skull and crossbones flag. A ragged cheer went up. I thought I should probably say something, some auspicious words, a farewell to the captain. Something. But I was never one for speeches. I looked at Patty. She didn't look inclined to talk either. Gruff hoisted the flag. I wanted to object, didn't they realise that being sighted by an Inquisition ship was going to be risky enough? Displaying the skull and crossbones was asking for their cannons to turn our way.

It was a long journey. We had time to become familiar with each other, if not family. I spent most of my evenings with Chani, practising the voodoo arts, and my days with Patty, learning to be a sailor. MacLaine was effectively captaining the ship. The others looked up to him. He was fair and kept the wind in our sails. They couldn't ask for more. It wasn't about plunder or riches or treasure this time, it was about survival, and they knew MacLaine would keep them alive.

Patty wasn't herself. She was withdrawn. Quiet. She lost herself in hard labour. The only concession she took was moving into what would have been Steelbeard's quarters. She was, after all, the captain's daughter, and Steelbeard would always be the captain of this crew.

The days stretched on.

We didn't catch sight of another vessel on the sea, and mercifully, didn't encounter the Kraken or any of its type.

After two weeks at sea the cry went up, 'Land ahoy!'

Within a few hours I could see the harbour, and the masts, and then in one sickening hour watched as the ships came out to greet us. One after another their gun ports opened and cannons rolled into place. They recognised our lines, how could they not? We were in an enemy vessel sailing into the heart of their safe haven. Why should a black flag bearing the skull and crossbones make any difference to them? The Inquisition could fly the pirate flag just as easily as any pirate crew. I fervently hoped they'd give us long enough to explain ourselves before turning their guns on us.

'Mister MacLaine,' I called across the deck. 'I suggest you assemble the scurviest bunch of sea dogs we have on board and get them up on deck so our friends can see we're not the enemy.'

'Aye, Cap'n.' The old helmsman said, clapping his hands.

One of the cabin boys scampered off to spread the word and within a few minutes the roughest of Steelbeard's crew lined the guard rail.

All that we could do now was trust that someone on the pirate ships recognised our boys in their telescope lens and called off the guns.

It was a tense hour as we drifted closer to the harbour, and then a pilot boat was dispatched to bring us in to anchor. We were greeted by roaring cheers when MacLaine and the lads took a bow. MacLaine was smiling, enjoying every bit of the acclaim as the audacity of stealing a ship from the Inquisition sank in. By the time we finally made our way ashore, there was a welcoming committee in place. These were MacLaine's people. Most of them, I realised, had known Patty since she was a young lass sat on their knees as they sang bawdy shanties to her.

There was a lot of beer and rum drunk that night, though I don't think I saw a drop pass either Chani or Patty's lips. I made up for them, of course. The one thing I was good at was drinking.

MacLaine told the tale of the daring theft at least a

dozen times, and each time it became more staggering a feat of derring-do. With each telling came another drink, and with each drink another dash of mettle to the tale. By the end of the night I was quite the hero.

When morning came though, I couldn't have felt less heroic.

I woke sprawled out on a bench in the inn, having passed out mid-drink. My skull felt too small and my brain too big. My tongue was twice the size of my mouth. It had been a good night.

I wanted to crawl back to the ship and sleep it off, but the longer we waited before we asked, the less likely it was that we'd be able to get any news of Slayne or Garcia that was worth hearing, and I was a man obsessed with keeping my promises to Steelbeard. I couldn't explain it, not rationally, but the longer I spent in his place the more determined I was to live up to his memory – or the crew's memory of him. And, of course, the longer we were here, the more time the Inquisition had to track us down. We had the Titan Harpoon. That single fact guaranteed that the Inquisition would do everything they could to find us. And Sebastiano was just vain enough to lead the charge. I half expected him to catch up with us, twirl his moustache and say, 'So, we meet again,' he was that kind of man.

Sooner or later, if they didn't catch us themselves, they'd try the next best thing and put a reward too big for any pirate to refuse on our heads, including a pardon, to hand us over. They wouldn't honour the pardon, of course, but that wouldn't stop some greedy pirate turning on us. Yes, I knew only too well how the Inquisition thought.

Patty had no sympathy for us drunks.

MacLaine was slumped against a wall with no immediate sign of him moving until Patty, having tried the incentive of a boot to the backside, threw a jug of water over his head. He came too, spluttering and gasping for breath as he shook his head. Patty didn't laugh.

In turn I accepted my soaking with good grace – and a few well-crafted curses – and when I opened my eyes I saw a particularly ugly little fella staring at me intently.

'What's the matter *dog-breath*? Never seen a gnome before?'

I looked the little guy up and down. There wasn't a lot to see. He primped though, like some strutting peacock. It wasn't that I had never seen a gnome before, more a case of not trusting someone I could throw that far. But this wasn't a place exactly founded on trust, so he was no better or worse than the rest of them.

Us, I amended.

'Sorry,' I said, not quite sure what I was apologising for, but it seemed expected.

'Apology accepted,' the gnome said, slipping down from his stool. He stumped his way towards me on short legs and held a hand outstretched. I moved tenderly so that I was at least half-sitting when he reached me. The taproom started to swim alarmingly before my eyes. I shook his hand. It was impossible to guess how old the gnome was, and I couldn't just cut him open and count the rings like a tree. He looked young, but that's such a relative thing inter-species. He could have been fifty years older than me.

'Jaffar?' Patty said, grabbing the gnome by the collar and hauling him up off the ground. It wasn't a hug. She was shaking him like she was trying to make something rattle free. 'Give it back, you thieving little toad.'

The gnome smiled ruefully and reached inside his shirt. He handed a meagre purse of coins to me. It took me a groggy moment to realise it was the same purse that had hung from my belt not so long ago. 'Can't blame a lad for trying,' the gnome said. I resisted the temptation to cuff him, as he'd probably have toppled from here into tomorrow and all the way through a month of Sundays. Besides, there was rarely more than the price of a meal, and if I was feeling particularly flush, a couple of drinks in there. This morning was no exception. Despite drinking my fill, and Patty's, and probably Chani's as well last night, I hadn't dipped my hand into my purse once. The pirates loved me. I was a bloody hero to them. I'd struck a telling blow against the Inquisition. I'd humbled Sebastiano, and in doing so honoured Steelbeard. Yeah, I was a hero in a den of thieves. Hardly surprising one of them had lifted my money.

'You know this little shit?' I said. Jaffar's stubby little legs kicked against thin air. I enjoyed the frustration growing in his face.

'Unhand me, woman! Let me go!' he shouted. 'I've given it back. What more do you want? Blood?'

'That doesn't make it right though,' I said. 'Patty? Can I take him off your hands? I think I'd like to wring his scrawny little neck and see what else falls out.'

'No need,' she said. 'He's probably got half of the settlement secreted in one pocket or another, has our Jaffar. And by our, I mean that last night I heard him trying to pass himself off as one of our crew to any woman daft enough to listen.'

'I like women. Especially when they're taller than me,' the gnome said, grinning at Patty.

I laughed. I admit it. I couldn't help myself.

He turned his attention on me.

'Are you the captain of the ship? The Inquisition one?'

'He is,' said Patty for me. I wouldn't have said so myself. I hadn't earned the title. As far as I was concerned, MacLaine was the man. I was just the liberator.

'They say that *you* used to belong to the Inquisition. That true?'

'Interesting way of putting it. So, what if I did?' I asked. I had no great wish to be reminded of my past, not when it was so recent, and to be honest when I was still so bitter about having a new life-path thrust upon me. But unwelcome or not, I owned my past, just like everyone else. And this wasn't exactly the sort of place I expected to be judged for who I had been rather than who I was.

'Just wanted to be sure, you understand? Bit of a legend, you. Let me introduce myself properly. No need to stand on ceremony, or dangle like this, as it were. I am indeed Jaffar and I am on a quest.'

'Are you now?'

'Indeed I am. I seek something perilous, a treasure most awesome, a deed beyond merely heroic, something that will prove my worth to the others of my kind. I seek something beyond compare, against impossible odds.'

'Really? That sounds… difficult. What, if I may ask, is it that you're looking for?'

'A name for myself,' the gnome said with a wry grin.

I couldn't help it, I found myself liking the rogue.

'That's some quest,' I said. 'So, where are you going to start looking?'

'Oh, I'm looking, I'm looking. Ever the opportunist. Can't not look. You never know when you might happen upon something heroic that needs to be done, and needs a small man to do it. Of course, it'd help to actually have my feet on the ground, eh, Patty?' The gnome pointed to the floor and waggled an eyebrow. Patty laughed and dropped him. Jaffar landed a little awkwardly. 'Thank you, m'dear. Now, what was I saying? Oh yes… see, I have an idea. You strike me as the kind of man trouble's attracted to, so the best chance of me making a name for myself is by sticking close to you. Simple.'

'Is that so?'

The gnome nodded eagerly.

'And why would I want to let you travel with me?'

'I have skills,' the gnome said, waggling his fingers again. There was no doubting he'd lifted my purse without my noticing, but I'm not sure I was quite ready to admit I needed someone with light fingers on my side.

'What the little bastard's not saying is that there's not another captain who'll have him within a mile of their ship,' MacLaine said. The helmsman stretched out, checking one of the tankards in front of him for a hair of the dog. I liked his style.

'And why would that be?'

'Because he's a no-good thief, of course, Cap'n. It's a miracle he hasn't had his hands cut from his wrists many times over–'

'Can only have them cut off once, old man,' Jaffar objected, as though that minor technicality actually made a difference.

MacLaine ignored him. 'It's only because he's inch high to a grasshopper that he gets away with it.'

'So you don't think we should take him with us?' I asked.

'Why should it matter what he thinks?' Jaffar put in. 'You're the captain.'

'You *are* the captain,' MacLaine agreed with the gnome. 'And as such, you decide who travels with us and who doesn't.'

'Do I also get to say who washes the lavatories and who gets thrown overboard?'

'Of course,' said MacLaine, smiling as though he

could read my mind.

'Good. Then I think I know exactly how our light-fingered friend can go about beginning to make a name for himself.'

'Anything you want me to do, I'll do it, boss,' Jaffar said.

'You'll have to earn your keep,' I said.

'Of course, of course.'

'And that means getting into the places a bigger man might find uncomfortable.'

Jaffar nodded. 'Wise. Yes. Makes sense.'

'Like the lavatories.'

'Yes,' Jaffar said. Then seemed to realise what he was agreeing to. 'Erm. No. Maybe. Erm. How about the rigging? I'm light on my feet and don't mind heights. Born climber.'

There was, of course, another way the young gnome could prove useful. I hadn't noticed him in the bar on the previous evening, despite his appearance. He was a thief. Thieves needed to be discreet. Unseen, unheard. He was small enough to remain almost invisible in a crowd. And while he was unseen and unheard, he'd both see and hear things. Maybe we could be of use to each other, after all.

'I need information.'

'I'm full of it,' Jaffar said, helpfully.

'I bet you are,' MacLaine grumbled. I barely hid my smile. It doesn't do for a pirate captain to smile too much.

'I'm looking for two men.'

'Maybe I know where they can be found?' Jaffar said.

'Maybe you do,' I agreed.

'Who are they?'

'They go by the names of Slayne and Garcia.'

'The captains? Oh my… Like I said, trouble. You've got yourself a bad habit of looking for it.'

'Here's my offer. No lavatories. No monkey runs on the rigging. If you can find them then the berth's yours.'

The gnome grinned broadly. 'Captain, my captain,' he said, 'I already know where Slayne is. He's on the Island of Thieves.'

'And just how do you know that?'

'Because that's where I left him.'

'You left? I thought a little runt like you would be right at home there,' said Patty.

The gnome sniffed and adjusted his clothes slightly, fixing his collar. He looked like someone trying desperately to regain a little of his dignity as he confessed, 'They said I wasn't *gifted* enough.'

And now I understood why it was so important for

the little guy to make a name for himself. He wasn't just a thief, he was a *bad* thief.

'Ever thought of a different occupation?' I asked.

'That's what I'm doing,' he said, earnestly. 'I'm becoming a hero.'

# CHAPTER 21

The gnome disappeared for most of the rest of the day. I was starting to think that he wouldn't be coming back.

MacLaine had shaken off the results of the previous night's excesses and had the crew hard at it, getting the ship into some semblance of order. He made adjustments here and there and disposed of anything that marked the ship as an Inquisition vessel. He wanted to replace the figurehead on the bow, and while we didn't have time to wait for a shipwright to carve something, we had money aplenty, so I took a trip down to the docks and ordered something for our return. Most ships sailed with beautiful women pointing the way, but we'd sail with Steelbeard's ugly mug looking out for us. It was only fitting. I arranged for sufficient supplies to be brought on board. More than sufficient, actually, my crew would all live like kings for a month, after that we'd make do. If there was an 'after that' to worry about. Patty had found the gold in a chest in Sebastiano's cabin. The man wasn't one for living like a pauper, even at sea.

One other perk of stealing the Commandant's ship was the flintlock pistol that now nestled on my hip. I had missed my gun. It felt good to be armed, properly. I felt ready to face anything.

Jaffar returned just as the sun crested the horizon. Most of the crew were going ashore for a final night of revelry and to work out any last frustrations before we set sail on the morning tide. I didn't begrudge them it for a minute, months at sea could get mighty lonely.

'Anything for me then?' I asked as the gnome plonked himself down on the bench beside me.

The gnome shrugged, and I knew he was going to make a performance out of it. I'd met his type before, and it seemed they came in all shapes and sizes. 'Slippery soul, that Garcia is,' Jaffar said. 'The whisper is that he and his men ambushed an Inquisition expedition to Maracai Bay. And by ambushed, I mean, *squelch*.' He drew a finger across his throat to support the none too subtle sound effect. I knew full well what he meant.

'Okay. Where is he now?'

Again that shrug. 'Not sure but I did happen to overhear a certain someone's conversation, and the gist of it seemed to be that Garcia had a bee in his bonnet about finding the Fire Temple.' Jaffar rolled his eyes as he said it, expecting us to mock. There was no mockery from me. It made a horrible sort of sense. We'd destroyed the Earth Temple and had been tasked with finding the lost Water Temple. I half-expected Jaffar to tell me next that Slayne had set sail for the Air Temple.

I turned to Patty and MacLaine.

'What do you think?'

They both knew the sea far better than I did. MacLaine had heard some of Steelbeard's final words, and what he hadn't heard from the captain, he had heard from us. He had already known Steelbeard's plans. I suspect that, right up until those final moments, he was the only person in the world the old pirate had confided in.

He scratched at the nape of his neck, and then lifted his eyes to the darkening sky. 'We go after Slayne first. Stands to reason. We know where he is, and if we're not capable of dealing with him, we shouldn't be going after Garcia. Slayne's also closer. He'll be easier to find.'

Everything he said made sense. I looked to Patty. She didn't disagree.

'The Island of Thieves it is then, though we might want to keep Jaffar here hidden, just in case they try to steal him from us.' I ruffled his hair – at least the part of it sticking out from beneath his floppy hat – earning a snarl from the gnome.

'We'll be ready to sail on the morning tide,' MacLaine assured me. 'I've warned the lads that we'll sail whether they're at their posts or not.'

After last night I expected us to leave the harbour with half of the men missing, but I shouldn't have doubted MacLaine. Steelbeard might have been dead, but the discipline and loyalty he instilled in the men lived on in his helmsman.

Still surprisingly sober – sobriety being a relative state for some of them – each and every one of them returned in time to get a few hours precious kip before we hoisted up our sails.

There wasn't a man who wanted to risk not being part of what happened next. These guys lived for adventure. And as Jaffar had pointed out, I had a way of finding trouble. The two went hand-in-hand.

I slept fairly well that night, even without wine to

help counteract the swaying of the sea beneath me. I have no idea if I was becoming inured to it, or just coming to terms with the idea that it would be my home, so I might as well get used to it.

The luxury of the captain's cabin didn't hurt though.

By the time I woke, morning had already broken rather ingloriously, with rain sheeting down from the sky. The deck was a hive of activity as men battled the elements to make the final preparations necessary for us to start the run to the Island of Thieves.

# CHAPTER 22

You can guess that with a name like the Island of Thieves this was another one of those charming places the Inquisition tended to stay the hell away from. More than once in my lifetime there had been attempts to establish some sort of official presence there, but every time it had just petered out. For any thief, stealing from the Inquisition was a victimless crime, after all.

We had been at sea for days. Without knowing where we were going, I found myself wondering if we'd managed to miss the island. MacLaine just smiled wryly and assured me that we were on course, and we'd see land soon enough. I don't know how these guys did it, going days on end without a single fixed point on the horizon that wasn't rocking or swaying. For me, that way lay an acute form of seasick madness.

We had seen sails on the horizon, and for that very reason deliberately changed tack so that we could avoid coming too close to any of them. No point risking being recognised or engaged. For now.

Jaffar was a constant irritant. He just didn't know when to shut up. He was even more clueless when it came to the whole making himself scarce thing. He just kept popping up at the most inopportune moments, earning regular threats of being thrown overboard. Some of the men took to calling him Bait, short for Kraken Bait. He didn't seem to appreciate the joke. I tried to tell him it meant he'd been accepted as part of our very unorthodox family. I kept my word, though. Even when he was at his most annoying, I hadn't sent him to clean the lavatories. Yet. But there was still time.

The cry of 'Land ahoy!' saved him from any of the dirtier jobs I might have dispensed.

MacLaine pulled his collapsing brass telescope out of his pocket, and surveyed the coastline. 'It looks like the little runt wasn't making it up after all,' MacLaine said, offering me the spyglass. I looked, but I wasn't sure what I was looking for. 'You see the ship with the light blue sails?' I nodded. There were more than half a dozen at anchor, but only one without a pearly white sailcloth. They were in the process of being taken down, but it was still easy to see the difference. 'That's Slayne's ship. He thinks it makes him harder to spot on the horizon, meaning he can get in close to his victims before he's spotted.'

It sounded reasonable, but what did I know? 'Is he right?'

'Depends on the weather, and just how blind the lookout is, but he must get more days when it's to his advantage than not, even if it looks like some god-awful vanity on his part. Anyway, we're in luck, it looks like being a rowdy night dockside tonight. You can always trust pirates to carouse up a storm when they hit dry land.'

'Predictable is good.'

MacLaine nodded. 'That it is. He'll know we're coming, which can't be helped. That also means most of his mob will have finished their duties and already headed ashore. But not Slayne. He's a real loner. Rarely mixes with his crew on dry land, hell, rarely sets foot on dry land. And he's a creature of habit. My money says we'll find him on board. I doubt he'll be alone though, he's paranoid enough to have a few men watching his back.'

'In other words he's not an idiot,' I said, which was true. If I was a pirate captain there's no way I'd send the crew off and sleep alone on an empty galleon. If… I had to stop thinking like that. I *was* a pirate captain, and not only in name. I wasn't sure about sneaking aboard his ship, though. It felt a little too much like walking into the lion's den, guards or not.

'Do you have any idea what the particular bounty you're expecting to find is?' MacLaine asked. We had all learned to be very careful how we talked about our business, especially if there was even the slightest chance little ears might be listening in. Most of our boys had been with Steelbeard for years and MacLaine trusted every one of them with his life, but he made a point, more than once, of telling me he wouldn't trust them with his daughter. But then, he didn't have a daughter.

Jaffar, well, let's just say Jaffar and trust weren't exactly on speaking terms and leave it at that.

We drifted into the harbour as the sun was setting. There was little wind. The bluffs sheltered the harbour from the worst of it. Gulls circled overhead. They cawed and cried. A fishing trawler was in. The men were gutting the day's catch on the waterfront. The taverns and inns would be well stocked tonight. The lights were on in a dozen of them along the harbour. The place was full of noise. Alive. There were girls leaning on the sea wall, waiting to welcome my lads ashore. The ships already at anchor had little more than the occasional lantern burning to mark their position. The island was, to all intents and purposes, just like any other island we could have sailed in to. It had a thriving populace. It had cooks and cobblers and vintners and shopkeepers. It had chandlers and bakers and whores. In other words, it was my kind of town.

We dropped anchor. The entire crew stood on deck with me, watching in silence. Slayne's ship was in full view but there was no sight of anyone on board.

It was Patty who eventually broke the hushed silence by asking, 'Why do you think he is here of all places?'

It was a fair question. I'd wondered about it myself plenty of times during the journey. He had to have a reason. If I'd understood Steelbeard correctly, the captains were all under a compunction. They were forced to do Mara's bidding. So what did the demon want here? What was special about this place?

'He's a creature of habit. Most pirates are.' MacLaine explained. 'This is one of his supply points. You go where you know. That's how you stay alive in this game. Slayne has people he trusts here.' This had been MacLaine's life for so long I didn't doubt for a minute that he knew the ins and outs of a number of pirate vessels and the habits and haunts of their captains.

'But why *here*? Why here *now*? There are plenty of suppliers in the vicinity, there's Antigua for a start.' Patty said.

'Because there's something here he needs,' I said. 'And what would he need that he couldn't just buy or steal elsewhere?' They looked at me like I was speaking in tongues. 'Something from his stash,' I said. I couldn't tell you how I made the leap of logic with so little information, but as soon as I said it, I knew I was right. This was where Slayne hid his plunder.

'Hiding stolen property amid a bunch of thieves? He's either a mad man or a genius,' Jaffar blurted out, clearly enjoying the idea. 'You'd think it's the most dangerous place in the world, but what's the cardinal rule? Eh? You don't crap on your own doorstep.' He was right. And for that I didn't clout him around the ear for insinuating his way into a private conversation. There was no such thing as far as the gnome was concerned.

'The wee man's got a point,' MacLaine agreed. 'No one here would dare steal from one of their own. If they did they'd be putting their entire community at risk, and it's not worth it, no matter how pretty the trinket.'

'So if you were him, what would be the first thing

you did when you went ashore?'

'Check it was still there,' MacLaine said without missing a beat. 'Trust only goes so far.'

I smiled. Maybe I wasn't going to be so bad at this pirating caper after all. 'My thoughts exactly. You said he doesn't go ashore much. I'm guessing it's to check on his hoard, add any new acquisitions to it, and that's about it.'

'So we follow him, and we help ourselves to the ah… item.'

'Are you ever going to tell us what it is you're actually trying to find?' Jaffar asked.

'I doubt it,' I said.

A light moving on the deck of Slayne's ship caught our attention. We all held our breath. This was it. The decking creaked and groaned. The mast pulled at the timbers. The tide sloshed up around the hull. I could hear every single sound, my senses working overtime. The crew were already carousing in the taverns, telling tall tales, getting drunk and chasing skirt, which meant that the lone figure descending the rope ladder to the rowing boat bobbing against the side of the hull was almost certainly Slayne himself.

'You've got the luck of a pirate, Cap'n,' MacLaine said. I didn't point out the problem that Slayne was also a pirate.

Slayne hooked his lantern onto a support in the landing boat.

I started down for one of our own boats. The crew looked to me expectantly. They were waiting for me to give the order. Part of me wanted to take them all with me, but the more people who came ashore, the greater the chance of discovery. We had to assume our enemy was at least as good as we were. That way we wouldn't get sloppy and make stupid mistakes because we'd underestimated him. I knew the others would listen to me, but not Patty. She was coming with me whether I wanted her there or not. I didn't even try to dissuade her.

It wasn't going to be easy. We had to follow him without a lantern. We couldn't risk him seeing the light dogging his footsteps. I took MacLaine aside for a moment and whispered, 'I need you to stay here. If we don't come back you know what you have to do.' He nodded. He didn't look particularly happy at being sidelined, but he understood it was imperative the mission go on even if we weren't part of it. Some things are bigger than two people.

I didn't bother promising that we'd both return safely.

We were both men of the world. We knew the risks.

So we followed Slayne.

Instead of heading directly to shore, he angled the little rowing boat around the rocky promontory and up the coast, keeping out of sight of the last of the settlement's lights. We could see his lantern bobbing up and down in the darkness to the sound of the splash of his oars, leading us on into darker water like some corpse light looking for a way into the underworld. It gave me the creeps.

I tried to keep our distance, but it was difficult with the undertow carrying us faster than I would have liked. Even so, any noise we made shouldn't carry. I hoped. And if it did, then I hoped Slayne wasn't paranoid enough to be listening out for it. My arms burned from the exertion, and my breathing grew increasingly short and shallow as I pulled on the oars. We'd gone a mile and more before his boat finally stopped moving.

Slayne pulled it up onto the pebbled shore.

This was the most dangerous part of the night. I angled our own boat towards the beach, and kept each stroke shallow as we neared the stone beach. I couldn't risk dragging the boat all the way out of the water because of the noise it would have made. I just had to hope it wouldn't drift too far. There was a whole lot of hope going on. Cloud cleared from the moon for a moment. I caught sight of Slayne looking around, checking that he wasn't being followed. He didn't see us.

Patty and I waited in silence.

We didn't move for fear our boots would slip in the pebbles and shells and betray us. I would have killed for a sandy beach. When we finally started to walk each step we took threatened to give us away. I gave Patty a silent signal, gesturing towards the tree line. We moved fast and low. The tide covered the crunch of pebbles. Once we were off the stones we hugged the trees as best we could. The grass was deep and spongy, filled with moss that muffled the sound of our footsteps. We kept Slayne in sight all the way. He looked back in our direction twice before disappearing into the trees. For one heart-stopping moment I thought for sure he'd seen us as he raised the lantern and seemed to stare straight at us, but he lowered it again and plunged into the trees.

The lantern, of course, had saved us. It ruined his night vision. He was essentially blind beyond the reach of the light.

We followed him into the trees. We had to quicken our pace so that we did not lose him as the vegetation thickened. We got lucky. Patty caught sight of him pushing back heavy scrub and disappearing into a cave entrance. If she hadn't seen it, we'd have lost him. The cave was virtually invisible thanks to the overgrown scrub and the night, which turned everything various shades of black.

We crept closer, straining to hear anything coming from inside the cave.

We reached the bushes without being challenged.

Patty held the vines back so that I could slip through into the cave. I could see the faint glow of Slayne's lantern deep inside. The cave was much bigger than I'd expected. The passageway was too narrow for me to draw my sword, but it was perfect for the flintlock. I drew the pistol and thumbed back the hammer. It was so tight I had to squeeze in sideways. Patty followed a few feet behind me. I heard the loud rustle of the vines and scrub dropping back into place behind her. It carried strangely in the tight confines of the cave, seeming impossibly loud. I winced. We edged our way deeper into the cave, though I was thinking of it more as a deep crevice now, and not a cave at all.

The light was always in front of us, guiding us.

Finally, after what felt like an eternity of my face pressed up against bare rock, the passage opened into a larger cave.

There was no sign of Slayne.

His lantern hung invitingly on an iron spike.

Pushed into one corner of the cave were a number of wooden chests bound with iron bands and held secure with great padlocks. So we'd found the treasure, just not the man. I could live with that if it meant we could grab the dagger and get out of there before he came back from wherever he'd gone.

I hurried over to the chests. I had no idea what the Sacrificial Knife looked like, or how I would recognise it amidst his hoard of gold, trinkets, gems, and other stolen treasures. Would it have some sort of *presence* like the harpoon? Would it *thrill* beneath my fingertips, full of magic? Would it beckon to me, willing me to pick it up?

I didn't have a chance to find out.

'Well, well, well, so eager to die young are we?' a voice called from the passageway. 'Take a good look around, familiarise yourself with your tomb. You're going to have eternity to enjoy its comforts.'

'Slayne,' I said, earning myself a wry chuckle from the pirate.

'Who else were you expecting to find here? This is my cave after all, and these are my treasures amassed over years of plundering. Tell me, honestly, did you really think it would be that easy to steal from me?'

Actually, I had, but I didn't think he wanted to hear that.

'We only want the knife. You know which one,' Patty said. I wished she had kept her mouth shut. Right up until then he only knew for sure that I was in here. She'd just told him there were two of us. So any hope of her surprising him just went right out of the window – or cave mouth, so to speak. 'It doesn't have to end badly.'

'Oh, I think it already has. I know that voice. Steelbeard's little girl. Won't you join us?' I still couldn't see him. I had a bad feeling about this. 'And that must make *you* the Inquisition spy sailing with Steelbeard? It's all rather charming that you think you'll save the day. Even if you had been able to assemble the artefacts, you would never be able to find the Water Temple, even if the traitor Steelbeard gave you directions. It was not yours to find, lad. No. As far as you are concerned it would always remain hidden. So really I'm just saving you a world of pain and disappointment.'

I heard the sound of footsteps above me. They could have been behind me. The acoustics were weird. All it meant was that my gun wasn't going to help if I couldn't see the man to shoot him. I didn't know where he was hiding, but there were obviously a number of tight passageways leading in and out of this central cavern like spokes from a wheel. And then I felt rather than heard the shifting of stone on stone. There was nothing good about that sound. Far from it. There was a lot of *bad* about that sound. The entire cave shivered and trembled until dust and debris fell from the roof.

Patty hurried towards me. I thought for a moment she was going to throw herself into my arms. We both knew that this was it; our last stand. Rocks broke away and fell to block the passageway. The collapse sent a cloud of dust our way. Coughing and choking, I covered my mouth with my sleeve. I grabbed Patty and held her close for all the good it would do.

I saw the dark streak of a fissure opening up in the stone above my head.

Once the roof caved in there would be nothing I could do to save her.

I kissed her.

I'd wanted to do it forever, and if I was a dead man, well I was going out with one glorious memory on my lips right at the end. It was a deep, perfect, passionate kiss right up until the moment she pushed me away.

'We're not dying yet, idiot,' she said. 'So keep your

bad breath to yourself for now.'

Then the world fell silent.

# CHAPTER 23

She was right. We weren't dead.

I was beginning to think I was unnaturally lucky. This narrow escape stuff was getting to be a bad habit. Or maybe it was a good one?

I have no idea how long we lay in the dark. The lantern had smashed as it hit the cave floor. Slayne couldn't have planned it, but it was the perfect final nail in the coffin as his trap fell into place. I had thought the entire cave was somehow rigged to collapse, but it wasn't, only part of the roof had fallen, sealing the passageway. It didn't make a lot of difference, really. It transformed a fast death crushed beneath tons of rock into a slow one. We were deprived of food, water and oxygen. There was no way we'd be able to clear the cave-in from this side, not the two of us alone. And, of course, I had given clear orders for MacLaine to set sail for Antigua if we did not return by daybreak. He was a good man, but he wasn't reckless in the same way that I was. He wouldn't risk more lives by defying me.

We had known full well what kind of danger we were going into. It was imperative the Harpoon was kept out of the reach of the Inquisition. It was as simple as that. I'd doomed the pair of us by thinking about the worst-case scenario, and then leading us into it.

But Patty wasn't about to sit down in the middle of the cave and give up without a fight.

She set to work clearing some of the boulders from the cave mouth. She worked by touch, at first hauling the stones free, then dragging the heavier ones, but she barely made any inroads on the collapse. I joined her. Two extra hands didn't exactly make light work of it, and we were burning through our air, breathing hard from the exertion, but frankly I'd rather go out doing something rather than sitting around counting my sorrows.

After an hour, two, three, four, it was impossible to tell because time lost all meaning in the dark, we'd cleared some of the loose rubble and opened a crack near the top of the cave-in, which in theory might – just might – have allowed enough air in for us to die of dehydration instead of suffocation.

I heard movement on the other side of the collapse and realised that MacLaine didn't listen to me any more than anyone else did. For once I was glad. 'Leave no man behind,' a voice piped up. I saw lips and a grinning face lit up like a death mask by the torch in his hand as Jaffar's entire head filled the small gap we'd managed to clear. I'd never felt so happy to see the little bastard, ever. I suspected that I never would again, either.

'Don't go dying on us now,' the gnome said cheerfully. 'This is the first step in me making a name for myself, saving the brave captain and the innocent maiden—'

'You're not talking about me, are you, Jaffar?' Patty said, sweetly. She was hardly anyone's definition of innocent, and it was one hell of a stretch of the imagination to think of her as a maiden.

The gnome sniffed, ignoring the reproach because it didn't suit the story he wanted to tell. 'When I saw that Slayne had returned to his ship, I went to find old grump MacLaine. We were on the deck when his men started to return. Nothing about that felt right, you understand? First day in port, shipping out before the night's done? Just doesn't happen. But it was. Slayne'd sent runners down to round them up. You could tell they weren't happy, either. But they did as they were told, and weighed anchor about an hour back.'

'Slayne's gone?' Patty asked.

'There was nothing for him to hang around for, was there? We were done for. All he had to do was wait us out. It would only be a matter of time before we died and his treasure would still be here when he returned.'

'But he didn't bank on me,' Jaffar said. I was grateful for the mountain of stone between us, otherwise I suspect the little guy would have come in for a big old hug and left with my purse, my gun, and anything else he could get his hands on.

The next few hours were driven by a new purpose. We were getting out. MacLaine and some of the men worked diligently on their side of the cave-in, we worked on our side, until we'd cleared enough of the debris away to be able to crawl over the top of it.

It turned out that MacLaine had only been able to find us because I was so careless. I'd left tracks a herd of wildebeest would have been proud of as I followed Slayne through the undergrowth.

Jaffar wriggled through the gap. His ridiculous hat spilled into the cave, with him tumbling after it a few moments later. He dusted himself down and looked up at me. I knew what he wanted. I ruffled his spiky fringe again, almost knocking his stupid hat off his head. That wasn't it.

He held his torch aloft. It was so bright I couldn't look directly at it. The gnome peered over my shoulder at the ironbound chests against the wall.

'Tell me that's Slayne's treasure,' he said. There was no hiding the delight in his voice.

'It certainly is, but before you go getting any ideas, thief, the *only* thing we are removing from this cave is the Sacrificial Knife, understood?'

'You must be joking,' the gnome said, rubbing his hands in anticipation of getting at the locks.

'No jokes,' Patty grabbed him by the collar and lifted him up so he could just about stand on tiptoes. 'We do not steal from each other, Jaffar. I'm serious. There is a code of honour between pirates. We do not take from our own. Ever.'

'And yet you are going to take some knife and that's okay is it? Tell me, is it encrusted with fabulous jewels? Is it so beautiful it would make the gods weep to look at? Or, let's cut the crap, is it valuable?'

'I doubt it very much,' I said, 'on all counts.'

Jaffar grumbled and extricated himself from Patty's

grasp. He pushed past me, stumping over to the chests on his short legs. The flickering torchlight showed thick layers of dust. There was no rubble on or around them. Slayne had clearly been very careful with his trap. MacLaine had been on the money; the guy was clearly paranoid. But in this case, we really had been out to get him.

'We'll need something to force the locks,' I said, but before I'd actually managed to say the word "locks" the gnome had popped the first one and was throwing open the lid of the chest. 'I'm a thief,' he said, defiantly. 'What? Didn't you think I'd be able to pick a lock? Sheesh, I'm wounded, I am. Wounded.' He didn't seem particularly wounded. Actually, he seemed rather delighted with himself.

The first chest was full to the point of overflowing with coins, all of them gold. I did not recognize the denominations of even half of them. I crouched down beside the chest and ran my fingers through them like they were water, while Patty held the torch so that I might better see. Beside me, Jaffar set about opening the second strongbox. He flung the lid back with a flourish, sending a fresh dust plume into the air; this one contained an assortment of jewels and golden cups and goblets and cutlery. I shouldn't have been surprised at the sight of golden knives and forks and spoons, but I was. It was just so… unnecessary. So ostentatious. Even before the gnome had opened the third box the vast fortune that Slayne had accumulated was there for all to see. These were riches beyond anyone's wildest dreams. Even the little thief's.

He tried valiantly to convince me that it was our duty to liberate it.

'We can't just leave this for anyone to find,' said Jaffar, unable to take his eyes from the mountain of gold coins. He picked up a handful and let them spill through his fingers like grains of sand. 'Think of all the good we could do with this? We could set up orphanages for pirate children,' he suggested, though I suspected the only orphan he had in mind was a certain gnome not too far from where I was standing. 'Or build our own settlement… in honour of your father,' he said, appealing to Patty. 'Call it Steeltown? I can see it now.'

'I'm sure you can,' she said.

'Jaffar's right,' I said, enjoying the way his face lit up. 'But that doesn't change the fact that we're not taking anything from here apart from the knife.'

'You're killing me!' he moaned.

'You wanted to be a hero, I didn't force you to be one.'

Jaffar sighed. 'I could grow to hate you, do you know that?'

'You wouldn't be the only one,' I said.

The dagger was in the fifth of the chests the gnome cracked open. I recognised it immediately – and not because it was beautiful or encrusted with stunning gemstones that made it priceless. Quite the opposite. But it was obvious it had to be the knife. When Jaffar threw back the lid on the fifth chest there was nothing but a simple knife with a wooden handle and flint blade lying alone on a bed of soft white sand.

I took the dagger from the box and stood up. I studied the blade in the flickering torchlight. Behind me MacLaine and the men continued shifting the rubble, opening the passageway. The knife was old. I mean *old*. The flint was stained dark with blood. How many victims had it claimed?

I heard a curse, muttered low and harsh. Patty. I did not understand the words but it was clear what they meant.

'Okay, job done. Let's get out of here,' I said.

'But. . . but. . . but. . . the treasure?' Jaffar said.

'Okay, my *friend*,' I said, the emphasis heavily on

friend, to prick his conscience, assuming gnomes had them. 'One question, think about it, and tell me the truth: is this it? Is this what you are looking for? The object of your quest? Is this how you'll make your name?'

The gnome looked at it then back at me, miserably. He shook his head. 'No.'

'I didn't think so.'

'But it could help me find what I'm looking for,' he said hopefully.

I shook my head.

MacLaine had cleared away a path for us to clamber through. He stood atop the rubble.

'Mister MacLaine,' I said, 'when we're out of here I'd like some of the men to come back with gunpowder and blow the entrance again.'

'I'll see it's taken care of,' MacLaine nodded in agreement. 'Who knows what curses Slayne has placed on this stuff.'

'Curses?' Jaffar said, letting another fistful of coins slip through his fingers. This time he wiped his hands on his jacket and then scurried away, putting as much distance between himself and the treasure chest as he could. 'If that's the case, why are we still here? We've got a quest to be about, gentlemen. And lady,' he said, nodding to Patty.

The little gnome was the first one out of the cave system, first back through the trees, first onto the beach and first back onto the ship. His little feet didn't stop running all the way. He didn't look back once.

We were a step closer to facing Mara; a step closer to avenging Steelbeard's death. And maybe, just maybe, I was a step closer to fulfilling my promises.

I could live with that.

# CHAPTER 24

Smoke was still rising in the wake of the explosions when we set sail.

Not a single soul had looked out from the taverns or the ships anchored in the bay. This was the kind of place where it didn't do to pry into someone else's business. Thieves lived outside the law, which meant that they were skilled at minding their own business and liked to keep it that way.

We had no need to go ashore for supplies. The stores were still overflowing thanks to the excess of Antigua. And despite the nearness of the brothels and taprooms none of the men complained too bitterly about not being able to tap the various opportunities dry land offered. But then, they hadn't been at sea for months. They were a good crew. They understood the dangers we were sailing towards, and the ones we were sailing away from. Soon enough I was going to have to tell them exactly what they'd got themselves into, it was only fair that they should know what they were letting themselves in for. But not until we were well away from here.

As usual, MacLaine had the men working quickly and efficiently, even in the dark. Their skill and discipline was a credit to the helmsman, and in no small part to Steelbeard himself. I rather liked Jaffar's idea about founding Steeltown in his honour. Maybe one day. MacLaine set our course by the stars. The only danger was that Slayne was hiding out there, running silently in the dark, cannons primed to bring us down as we left the safety of the harbour.

We doused every lantern and torch, sailing in complete darkness. Only the creaks of the mast would give our presence away. And Slayne would have had to be right on top of us to hear those. I wasn't familiar enough with the ship to find my way around in absolute darkness, so I was consigned below decks where I was least likely to blunder into something and give us all away.

And all the time I was down there it felt like I hardly dared to breathe.

But when the sun finally rose there was no sign of

any sails on the horizon, white or blue, or any other colour. The danger had passed. Or at least one of them had. I didn't for a minute think we'd seen the back of the Inquisition. And we still had to face Garcia.

The pirates worked tirelessly, driving themselves on even when tired muscles demanded that they should rest. I could well understand why Steelbeard was so feared. These men went beyond human endurance. They just kept tapping fresh reserves when mortal men would have fallen. I knew in some way it was because revenge drove them on. Steelbeard was lost and they wanted to come good for his daughter, even if he wasn't there to see it. Particularly because he wasn't. It was simple psychology.

Chani did her thing; skulking in shadows, brooding quietly and looking far too sexy for her own good. That woman was made to brood. I'm sure she was praying, or mediating or communing with her Voodoo forces. Mine is not to reason what or why, only to enjoy the fact she looked drop dead gorgeous doing it. I'm simple like that.

I spent my days at the keel, Titan Harpoon ready in case the Kraken should rise. I wasn't about to let it scupper us so close to our destination.

And that was all that mattered: reaching our destination.

We were all working to the same goal.

There was no great cheer when Maracai Bay came into view. The men had driven themselves beyond the point of exhaustion. They simply had no more to give. Not even a cheer. They focussed on the rest that would come with landfall. There would be no drinking and carousing tonight. But there would be time enough for that tomorrow if we didn't die in the meantime.

I gathered the men together. It was time to tell them everything. Starting with the fact that Garcia was almost certainly searching for the Fire Temple, and why.

I didn't even know how to find the Temple. There wouldn't be signposts. There were no maps. The best I could hope for was that there would be a well-travelled path, or a native guide we would be able to hire to lead the way. As plans went it was sketchy at best.

My heart sank as I saw the familiar lines of an Inquisition ship offshore.

My mind raced.

We were flying the pirate flag, but that could be changed easily enough. It all came down to whether or not they had men on board who had heard that I was exiled from their ranks. If not, there was a chance that I could blag it just long enough to buy us the time we needed, but it was one hell of a risk to take.

I would have much been happier if it had been Garcia's ship, even if its big guns were aimed at us, because at least then the last artefact would have been in sight. I gave the order to lower the black flag and replace it with the Inquisition insignia. The illusion wouldn't stand up to close scrutiny. I just had to hope it wouldn't have to.

There was a pair of Inquisition guards waiting on shore as we approached. I recognised one of them.

'You're a long way from home,' I said in greeting.

'The Inquisition's reach is growing longer,' he said. I had heard the line so often it had almost become a mantra. To be brutally honest, I wouldn't lose any sleep if I never heard it again.

'What brings you here?' I asked.

'We have been sent here to cleanse this place,' he said, the glint of fanaticism in his eye. 'Before this place becomes as infested as Antigua.'

'Pirates?'

The man nodded. That he hadn't given the order to clap me in irons as soon as he'd set eyes on me was reassuring. The reach might be long, but the left hand didn't have a clue what the right one was up to. I might just wriggle my way out of this mess yet. 'That is what we heard, Sir. Our captain suspects their ship is anchored nearby, the place is a warren of secret coves and hiding places all the way around the coastline.'

'But why here?' I asked, trying to keep my inquiry innocent enough.

'The treasures of the fabled Fire Temple, Sir.'

I raised an eyebrow at that. 'Chasing legends? How very. . . pirate-like. Tell your captain that I am more than willing to bring my men ashore and aid the purge.'

'I am sure that the Captain will welcome any assistance that you are able to offer, Sir.'

He gave me directions, pointing the way. I listened intently, memorising every twist and turn between here and the Fire Temple.

Then I gave the signal to the ship. The Inquisition flag came down. In its place the black skull and crossbones climbed the mast.

The look of surprise and then abject horror as the Inquisition guard realised what it meant was priceless. I held the muzzle of my flintlock to his throat. Patty pressed the blade of her knife up against his companion's throat. 'I don't want to hurt either one of you, understood?' Both men nodded. They didn't believe me, that much was obvious. 'I don't kill good men. You have my word. But

I can't risk you raising the alarm.'

We gagged them both and tied them to a tree.

'You'll be safe here,' I promised them. 'Just don't go and do anything stupid. Please.'

Their eyes were as wide as the gold doubloons we'd left in Slayne's cave. They looked very much like two men who would end up doing something stupid. I couldn't help them if they did.

MacLaine had the landing boats in the water and was bringing men ashore in a matter of minutes. Most of them, to be honest, were far too exhausted to be of much use. I didn't want them slowing us down. And it wouldn't take all of us to find Garcia. I sent two dozen of them back, with orders to rest because we may well have need of them to get us off the island – even if things went well.

I made another decision then, strength becoming the better part of valour in my reasoning. I sent all but four back to the ship.

Despite MacLaine's insistence I point blank refused to let him join me on the journey inland. He was every bit as exhausted as the rest of the men. More so, really. I couldn't recall the last time he had slept a night through. The reality was that only Patty, Chani and Jaffar were fresh enough – and only then because we had been consigned below decks during the silent running and ended up sleeping most of the night out. I set off in the lead, the others close behind me.

The path had been trampled so thoroughly even a blind man could have found it. We followed in the Inquisition's footsteps, who in turn had followed in Garcia's footsteps. It was like one elaborate game of follow the leader.

The guards had said we were about an hour behind the main party, but we could move faster. It was maybe fifteen minutes before I heard the first voices up ahead. We were still too far away to make out *what* was being said, but the *how* was obvious: the conversation was laced with laughter. Spirits were high. I raised a finger to my lips, commanding the others to silence. We crept along the path, moving as quietly as the carpet of broken branches would allow. We reached a clearing. Five Inquisition guards sat in a circle. They passed a bottle around, each taking a deep swallow before handing it off to the next man. Standards had slipped in some parts of the Inquisition, it seemed. Not that I could comment. Some men left a trail of broken hearts in their wake; I left a trail of broken bottles.

I took a deep breath. I looked around. I counted to eleven, one extra for good luck, and was about to step into the open, when it hit me: something was wrong.

While I could imagine a group of soldiers sharing a drink when their captain's back was turned – I had done it often enough – these men looked so *slovenly*. . . My mind raced. It was just *wrong*. If the guards on the beach had looked even half as dishevelled, then perhaps, but they hadn't been. They'd looked every inch the part, still disciplined soldiers. It dropped into place, but before I could say or do anything Jaffar shifted his weight on those stubby little legs of his and snapped a twig. It sounded like a musket shot.

One of the men glanced in our direction.

I hadn't noticed that this one was wearing a captain's uniform, but I had noticed he didn't drink from the bottle as it went around the circle. Patty whispered urgently in my ear. 'I know him,' she said. 'It's Garcia.'

She'd beaten my brain to it by a fraction of a second. I knew she was on the money. But that begged the question: if these were the pirates, then where were the guards?

I looked at the men more closely. There was damage to some of the uniforms. It was enough to make me think that five corpses were lying in the undergrowth.

Garcia looked in our direction again. I gritted my teeth and stepped into the clearing. I could blag it, I was sure. I had the advantage over them, I knew that they were not as they seemed, whereas they couldn't begin to know the same about me.

'Friends,' I said, clapping my hands together warmly. 'Damn but it's good to see some friendly faces in this hellhole! Genaro said I'd find you boys here. Hey, chuck us that bottle will you? A fella could die of thirst.'

'Genaro?' Garcia asked.

'The one and only,' I sold the lie. I might not look the part anymore, but I'd been an Inquisition man for a decade so I could at least sound the part. 'We go way back. Served together in Faranga with Mendoza, years ago. I was just surprised to see him left doing beach duty, but he pointed me in the right direction.'

'Ah, of course, *that* Genaro. Good man,' Garcia said, trying to sell his own lie. As if there'd be two men called Genaro in the same unit. There wasn't even one. But he didn't know that.

'So, any joy?' I asked, taking a deep swig from the bottle when it was offered to me. I passed it on to the next man. Close up, they looked like they'd been in one hell of a scrap. And now they'd drunk too much, I could take two before they'd even got up off their fat arses. Only Garcia looked like he'd put up any resistance. It was sloppy of him letting his entire crew blow off steam at once, no matter how safe he thought they were. Well, he'd pay for it.

'Not yet,' Garcia said. 'But I'm sure my boys'll be able to handle them if we come across the pirates. How about you?'

'I'm looking for a man.'

'Oh yes?' The way he said it made one of the more drunken men snicker.

'Garcia. Pirate captain. I've had word he may be on the island.'

Garcia looked at me then. He hadn't been able to mask the instinctive flicker of recognition at his own name. He wanted to see if I'd noticed it. I had, but that didn't mean he'd noticed that I'd noticed. Thinking about it made my head spin. 'I've heard the same,' he said, cautiously. 'You after him for a reason?'

'He has something I need.'

'A pirate? What could you need from him?'

We were both doing the dance now. One of us would slip up soon enough. I wished I'd given Patty my flintlock. She could have put a bullet between his eyes the minute it looked like he was going to give me trouble.

I waved a hand, 'It's of no great importance,' I said,

offhandedly. 'But I would be grateful if I could join you for a while? There's nothing to be gained from me stumbling around the wilderness on my own. How about we combine forces?'

'Of course. You're more than welcome. What of your men, will they be following?'

'Naturally, but when Genaro said you were up here, it seemed wise to make contact first. My crew will be following along.'

'As I said, you are welcome, but alas, we cannot afford to linger here too long.'

He pulled a leather bag closer to him. It was a curious gesture. I understood the implications of it, even if it was unconscious. He was bringing it within a protective distance. If he had the Bone Hand with him, it was going to be in that bag. His body language fairly screamed as much. I didn't even think about it; I clenched my fist. It would have been so easy. I saw it in my mind, perfectly choreographed; a straight left to the jaw, a knee driven up into the gut and as he doubled up, a crushing upper cut to put his lights out. He had four drunks to defend him. I had Patty and Chani. And Jaffar would be lurking somewhere close. He lurked a little bit too well for my liking, but it came in handy every now and then. Like now. It would certainly have been easier to take Garcia – and the Bone Hand – here than risk trying to attack his ship.

But I didn't swing.

Yet.

'Is there any chance that one of your men could head back along the path and keep an eye out for my guys?'

Patty and Chani would take care of him before he'd covered one hundred yards, of course, meaning I'd only have to worry about Garcia himself and three drunks instead of four. Every little helped.

'No problem,' Garcia turned to two of his men. 'Miguel, Faustino, see to it our new friend's men don't get lost.' The pair rose grumpily, obviously reluctant to leave, but they weren't about to disobey their captain, whether he was pirate or Inquisition. That he'd dispatched two men instead of one was a sure sign that Garcia did not see me as a threat.

The pair disappeared down the path.

I counted the seconds.

It took a little longer than I'd anticipated, but not much, then I heard the sounds of a scuffle. I smiled coldly. It was a wonder they'd not heard about the mad man with one eye that had taken over the helm from Steelbeard. The remaining two men set after them. Garcia didn't move.

He was sober enough to realise that the real danger came from me, not from invisible forces hiding in the woods.

He drew his sword in one fast fluid motion. The blade was long and wickedly curved. It looked hungry. I didn't intend to feed it.

It was just me and the pirate.

'Your breaths are numbered,' Garcia gloated, spinning the blade in his hand. It became a solid blur, it whipped around that quickly. I was tempted to reach for the gun and put a metal shot in his head, but the powder wasn't tamped, and there was no guarantee the flintlock would even fire. 'You might want to count them while you still can.'

'You talk too much, Garcia,' I said, drawing my own sword before he had closed the gap between us. I didn't waste any energy with pretty flourishes or trying to look intimidating, I dropped straight into a tight fighting crouch. He came at me. Steel clashed against steel, again and again and again. Each ferocious blow sent a shockwave stinging along my sword arm as I parried it. And each one stung my shoulder. It had been a while since I'd damaged it, but this was the first real test it had had since. Garcia was stronger than I was, no doubt about it. He delivered his blows like a blacksmith pounding on an anvil. I was the anvil. But I was faster than him; more agile. We traded another flurry of blows. Each one sapped another ounce of strength from me. I needed to trade on my speed. That meant taking a risk at some point, but that would be the only way I was going to walk away from this one.

We circled around each other, turning first one way then the other as I tried to find a gap in Garcia's defence.

There wasn't one, which was a bit discouraging.

I'd just have to make one.

I feigned a move to the left, selling it hard all the way down to the way I *almost* shifted my balance in my legs – every muscle telegraphed the move – but it never came. Instead I slid my blade inside his as he made to defend the phantom strike. He'd realised what I was about to do, but too late for his own blade to go deep into my arm. He did cut me, but it was a shallow slice instead of deep to the bone, and for my pain I drew blood from the side of his chest, my blade biting plenty deep enough to cause him real discomfort.

Garcia winced in pain and clutched the wound with his free hand.

That was the beauty of my cut – every single move he made now was going to cost him, and every single move would be considerably weaker than the last.

I could have moved in for the kill then, but instead I stepped back, showing too much compassion. He came at me again, this time with a dagger in his free hand. Now I had two blades to worry about. If he could get himself close enough to do some damage it was still quite possible this would end badly for me. But he was bleeding a lot. All I had to do was keep him at arm's length and time would work its poison on his body. He knew it and I knew it. Which was why he threw caution to the wind and hurled himself forward.

It was kill or be killed.

I saw the attack coming. It wasn't pretty. I danced to the side, narrowly evading being skewered, and sliced my blade into his midriff. He lost his grip on both weapons in that moment, hanging on the end of my sword for a long moment before he crumpled to the ground.

I stood over the dying man.

'It's over,' I said retrieving the leather sack and withdrawing the Bone Hand from inside. It was by far the most vile relic I'd ever had the displeasure of coming into contact with. I could understand all too well how it could taint a man's soul, even from this brief touch. There was dark magic here. 'The other Titan artefacts are in my possession, Garcia. I *will* destroy your mistress. You have my word on that; a promise to a dying man. Believe me, I take those very seriously.'

'You will never find her.'

'Like I didn't find you, or Slayne? It's what I do. I find people. And, to be honest, I tend to kill them. So why don't you make it easy on yourself and tell me the location of the Water Temple? Then I'll put you out of your misery.'

'Never.'

'I had a feeling you'd feel that way about it. Let me try and convince you.' I put my boot to the wound. Garcia cringed with imagined pain before I even made contact. It seemed a pity to waste it, so I drove my foot down, hard. He screamed. I waited for him to stop, then I asked again, 'Tell me the way to the Water Temple.'

'You'll never find it,' the pirate rasped through clenched teeth.

'People keep telling me that. They're wrong.'

I drove my foot down again.

Garcia screamed. This time when he stopped he cursed me with venom in his voice. 'You will *never* find it. But when she is free she *will* avenge me. She will strip the flesh from your bones and feed it to her children in the dark waters.' By the time the last few words escaped his lips it was clear that they would be his last. They weren't the worst I'd heard, but the fact he'd gone without telling me where the temple was really got my goat. I kicked him in the head, just because I could.

I slipped the Bone Hand back into the bag and slung it over my shoulder. Garcia was right, I may have had all four of the artefacts, but I still had no idea of where I needed to take them. The only people who could tell me where I needed to go were dead, apart from Slayne. All I could do was pursue him to the ends of the earth. Which I was quite prepared to do. As far as he was concerned, I was dead, so he wouldn't be looking over his shoulder. Hell's teeth, even if I hunted him down, there was no guarantee he'd spill the secret. None of the others had.

'You all right?' Patty asked, bringing me back to the here and now. I glanced across and saw that Jaffar and Chani were standing with her. The gnome had a small cut on his cheek. He wore the battle scar proudly.

'I'm good,' I said, hoisting the bag so they knew I had the hand.

'Look, this whole being clueless thing is no fun at all. Would someone *please* tell me what is going on?' Jaffar begged.

I looked at the others.

'I think you should,' said Patty. 'If it wasn't for him we might be dead, maybe more than once.'

'You can only die once,' I said.

'That shows what little you know,' Chani said in a voice so reverential it gave me chills.

We began the short walk back to the ship. On the way we put the gnome out of his misery. No, we didn't kill him. We told him about the Titan Artefacts. He already knew about the Kraken, but had thought it was just a story the pirates told to dissuade him from wanting to sail with them. I wouldn't have blamed them for making it up, to be honest. The little guy was an acquired taste.

'So what's in the bag?'

'A bone hand. *The* Bone Hand, to be more precise.'

'Seriously? Open up. This I've got to see.' I humoured him. The gnome peered into the leather sack, and whistled at what he saw inside 'That's seriously messed up. You know that? Carrying a dead guy's hand in a bag.'

'The problem is,' I said, 'We have to be inside the Water Temple to use them.'

'The Water Temple? That place is gone, right? Disappeared. Poof.'

'Lost,' I said, hoping that suggested it might be found

again. 'Steelbeard had been there, of course, as had the other captains.'

'But none of them told you how to get there?'

'That's why we have to find Slayne. He's the only one left who can tell us how to get there.'

'That is not so,' Chani said. I looked at her. Four men had been there. Three were dead. That left one who could tell us how to get there. 'He is not the only one.'

'I don't follow… The four captains are the only ones who have been there, right? And Slayne is the only one left alive.'

'Yes. He may be the only one *alive*, but that does not mean he is the only one you can ask.'

'You're doing my head in, Chani,' I said. I was tiring of her riddles. 'Spit it out. Please.'

'Captain Steelbeard knew the location of the temple.'

'Yes,' I said, doing my best to stay patient. It was like talking to a child.

'Don't you know what the Hand of Glory can do?' This time it was Chani speaking to me as though I were the child.

'The Hand of Glory?'

'The thing you call the Bone Hand has many names. It possesses powerful voodoo magic.' I wasn't about to argue with her, she knew her voodoo. 'With it you can travel to the Isle of the Dead. I can teach you how to enter the Underworld. Go there. Find the Captain's spirit. Get your answers.'

It sounded so simple. So reasonable. Travel to the land of the dead and talk to Steelbeard, why hadn't I thought of that? Oh, right, because it was mental.

But if I could speak to Steelbeard's spirit…

# CHAPTER 25

The Isle of the Dead was covered in thick heavy mist. MacLaine was sure we'd sailed around it several times before we had eventually stumbled upon it, and even then there was an element of luck in finding it. MacLaine turned the capstan while barking a rapid stream of orders; changes to be made to the sails, rigging to be adjusted, lines tightened or shortened. Chani had spent the last two days teaching me everything she knew about the island. I wish I hadn't heard half of it, but I couldn't *un*hear it. The single most important thing she told me was how to make contact with Steelbeard. The single most frightening thing she told me was what would happen if I angered the other spirits. I really didn't like the sound of being trapped down there forever. And I wouldn't be able to fight my way out if things got ugly.

'This is as close as I dare take the ship, Cap'n,' MacLaine said, finally.

'Then I guess this is it.' I'd already said my goodbyes. There was nothing to be gained from dragging it out. The hand gave protection to one individual. I had to do this alone. Chani and Patty had both offered to go in my place. They both had different reasons, but this was my promise to keep, not theirs.

So I boarded the landing boat and rowed for the island. With each stroke the temperature dropped. I felt the cold and damp chill me to the bone. The lantern that hung on the ship slowly disappeared until I was completely lost in the mist. There was no sun. The mist leeched out every sign of life from the world, taking with it every hope.

I glanced over my shoulder. I couldn't tell if I was closer to the island or not. The mist rolled on. I pulled on the oars. The gentle slap of the waves became the entire world. I pulled on the oars. It was cold. So very, very cold. It wormed its way into the very depths of me. And still I rowed on, until finally the bottom of the boat grated across the seabed. I clambered out, setting foot in the cold water. The chill seeped through my boots. I didn't think I could be any colder and still have blood pumping through my veins.

I pulled the boat well clear of the waterline. I didn't want to risk it being dragged back into the surf, leaving me stranded.

In this fog it was going to be hard enough to find my way back as it was.

I started to walk away, leaving the lantern burning in the bow of the boat and hoping it would help me to find my way back, assuming the oil reservoir was not used up by the time I returned. After twenty paces I turned, curious to see how well the lantern lit the mist. It was barely a faint watery glow. Great.

Chani had told me that I had to keep going until I had solid ground under my feet. I was still walking on sand when the lantern light finally disappeared from view. I tried to keep count of the number of paces I had taken, but had no idea if I was walking in a straight line. The mist was utterly confusing. Mystifying, I thought, and felt the giggle rising up. I swallowed it down. The lapping of the waves on the shore seemed closer than it had a moment before.

I walked on.

It grew colder still with each step. I was shivering and clenching my teeth.

The breaking waves seemed further away, finally.

I found myself wondering if this was it, the fate of an uninvited guest? To wander and wander endlessly in the mist?

I had nothing to lose. I took the hand from the bag, wondering what its protection would entail. I didn't expect it to lift the fog, but thought maybe it'd put an end to this otherwise endless wandering. The bone felt strangely warm to the touch. I almost dropped it in disgust, but then realised that it wasn't that it was warm, but rather that *my* hands were so cold it felt warm by comparison. That didn't make it any less disconcerting.

I held the Bone Hand out in front of me like some kind of offering.

The mist turned an eerie green around it as the hand began to glow gently. That sickly light illuminated my way. It was better than nothing. I took a step, then another and another, and then I felt something change underfoot. I had left the sand behind and was standing on solid ground. Little if anything seemed to grow here. There was no grass. There was no doubt in my mind that I had reached the place I needed to be.

I knelt down. I took the knife from my belt and began to gouge a scar in the earth.

I heard a scream with the first stab. I paused, trying to

hear where it had come from. Chani had warned me not to be distracted by strange noises, I had to finish what I started. I gouged the earth again, earning another scream, and again until I'd cut out a hole deep enough to take the whole blade. The cries spread. They were coming from every direction. If I listened too hard, I thought I'd recognise some of the voices, so I tried not to listen. That way lay the road to madness.

I emptied a small bottle of cockerel's blood into the hole and let it soak in before I spoke the words that Chani had taught me. I repeated them twice more before inserting the Bone Hand into the hole and speaking them again.

I trusted Chani. She said the charm would work. It would work. She said this incantation would open a doorway to the Underworld. It would open a doorway. I had faith.

The hand moved. Its skeletal fingers clenched, then flexed, finding life where there should have been none.

I wanted to run.

The cries stopped suddenly, as though silenced by the hand. It turned and twisted, bone grating on bone as it did so. I recited the remaining lines of the chant. The fingers moved in rhythm with the words, becoming part of the magic until at last the Bone Hand clicked its finger and thumb together and the mist shifted, swirling and gradually coalescing into shapes, human figures each of them distinct and recognisable in their own way.

And suddenly I understood. I hadn't been walking through a mist at all. This had been no fog. I had been walking through – and breathing in – the spirits of the dead.

Faces formed on the figures. A deathly pallor hung over them. I did not know any of them, not as a man, but I recognised them as the ghosts of pirates and Inquisition men, seafaring men all of them. More figures formed behind them; women and natives huddling together not knowing why they were in this place.

'Who have you come for?' All of the mouths opened and closed in unison. The ghosts spoke with a single voice.

I tried to speak but my mouth was dry. I couldn't say the name. Chani had told me that I would have one chance; that I could only save one person. The spirits shuffled and moved as others came to the front. I could feel them begging me to call their names even though I didn't know them. And then I saw the shades of men I had fought alongside. I saw my grandfather, long dead. I saw a boy I had known as a child. I had all but forgotten him. I felt guilty then, but who remembers a child killed by fever when they themselves were barely walking and talking? I felt their names rise to my lips. I wasn't about to say any of them though. I waited, knowing he would come to me.

Eventually I saw the streak of grey in his beard, the big man moving through the crush of spirits.

'Steelbeard,' I said at last, naming my dead, and the voices of dissent and complaint became overwhelming.

I covered my ears against the wails and the curses.

The spirits stepped aside and let the ghost of Steelbeard through.

'You came for me, lad,' he said. I nodded. There was nothing more to be said.

The other spirits began to drift again, dissipating into the mist they had come from.

I tried not to breathe the air now that I knew what I would be taking into my lungs.

The hand was still planted in the ground, but its fingers were no longer moving. I bent down to retrieve it, but as I did so it moved again, suddenly, and grasped me by the wrist. I couldn't break its iron grip and, try as I might, I couldn't pull it from the earth. It was as though it had taken root and was now part of the damned island, returning to the Underworld where it belonged.

In my excitement at having been united with Steelbeard's ghost, I had forgotten to speak the words of the second incantation, the one that would allow us to return. I pulled the bottle of spring water from my bag and sprinkled it liberally on the fingers, then spoke the second set of words. The hand fell limp, releasing its grip.

I took hold of it by the wrist and tugged it free of the ground.

This time it offered no resistance.

I slipped it back into the leather bag and hoped that I would be able to retrace my steps to the boat.

I needn't have worried. Steelbeard could see through the mist of spirits and led the way.

I followed.

The landing boat was where I'd left it, the icy cold waters creeping up towards its hull. I pushed it out into the water and clambered in. Steelbeard followed me. It was only when we were away from the island that he asked, 'So, hero, why have you come back for me?'

'You are the only one who knows the location of the Water Temple.'

I saw a twinkle in his dead eye.

I understood now why he hadn't finished his deathbed tale, the crafty old bugger.

# CHAPTER 26

I don't think I would have ever found my way back to the ship without Steelbeard.

His spirit drifted and shifted as he fought not to be sucked back into the mass of ghostly mist tattering in our wake. The fight took its toll on him. More than once his deathly pallor took on a strange luminescence, and with it, as the fog swirled around the dead man his eyes seemed to open up so that I could see straight through him. His body shifted in and out of transparency, but the harder I pulled on the oars, and the further we travelled away from the dead island, so the more substantial he became. Eventually the faint glow of the ship's lantern became visible.

'Do you know the danger you put yourself in, lad?'

I did, now. I hadn't understood before, even though

I'd thought I had. Chani's warnings hadn't come close to the reality of the situation. I looked at my friend, realising for the first time that was how I actually thought of the dead captain. Somewhere, the ghosts of a thousand Inquisition officers cried out in pain. 'It had to be done,' I said. 'There would have been more danger if I hadn't come here.' It was true, to an extent. Even if I had wanted to walk away I couldn't have done so. Fate had taken control of my life. Now I could only hope that it would help me defeat Mara. I really didn't want to be the kind of hero who fell at the final hurdle.

There was comfort in having Steelbeard alongside me in the landing boat, even if he didn't help with the rowing. And then I saw that the faint glow of the ship's lantern was gone.

'We're not free,' he said. 'The spirits will still try to stop me leaving.' I remembered the endless walk up the beach. I could well believe there would be some endless rowing, too. 'The Bone Hand may have given you safe passage, even offered protection, but it does not guarantee you will be able to take me with you. I am of this place now.'

'I know,' I said. 'But there is more to me than meets the eye.'

'I should hope so, otherwise I'd have to wonder what my little girl sees in you, lad.'

The mist was draining what precious little heat remained in my body. I put my back into the rowing, lifting and dropping the oars. After an eternity of cold, I leaned forward to the lantern and held my hands over it for warmth, rubbing them briskly before I took the oars again. It offered no comfort.

'Row, lad, row for pity's sake,' Steelbeard said. I saw that he seemed to have become part of the boat, some essential part of his spirit sinking into the wood itself. That was when I understood. Something was holding onto him, something below the dark waters, reaching up through the keel into our little tub, trying to keep him from escaping the island.

I pulled hard on the oars. The swell tugged us back. I pulled again and again, trying to build up momentum to push us from the grip of the tide, but the undertow was too strong.

Ghosts called from the mist. I saw them beginning to rise up from the water around us. Steelbeard started to turn. 'No!' One word was enough to stop him. We had to break the link between him and the other restless dead or he would be unable to leave. I had done so much to get him this far, but we were trapped in this no man's land between the shore and the deep blue sea. The dark waters. There had to be something I could do.

'Steelbeard,' I said, naming him. The power of the name was irresistible. It gave him something to anchor his soul onto. I said it again as I pulled on the oars and the boat started to slide through the water. Not easily, but we were moving. I called his name with every stroke, 'Steelbeard. Look at me. Steelbeard. *Look* at me. Steelbeard. . . ' My voice silenced the dead things that wanted him to stay.

The fog began to thin. I risked a glance over my shoulder, afraid that if I took my gaze away from the Captain I would lose him again, but we were out of the island's grip. The ship was closer than I had expected. Relief flooded through me as I heard voices on the deck, and Gruff's familiar voice announced our return.

We clambered back up the ropes onto the main deck.

Patty stood before us, rendered utterly speechless at the sight of her father returned from death. Finally, she moved, reaching forward to embrace him. Her arms passed straight through him. She stepped back as though bitten. She looked at me. I didn't know what to say. They would have time together, a chance to talk, which was more than they had managed before. It was a gift. She had to think of it that way.

MacLaine could barely restrain the smile that had spread across his face at the sight of his old friend.

Only Chani was interested in me. She moved up beside me, pulling back her hood as she interlaced her fingers with mine. 'Tell me all, every detail you can remember, tell me everything you heard. What did you see there?'

I didn't have any answers for her yet.

Jaffar was strangely quiet, keeping his distance from the dead man.

'There's nothing to be afraid of,' I promised, but the gnome quite obviously didn't believe me. He remained on the fringe of the celebrations as the rest of the crew rejoiced at having their real captain back on board. This may not have been his ship, but these were his men. It was one thing to follow MacLaine to the ends of the earth, but they would lay down their lives for Steelbeard.

I found myself hoping that one day I'd be able to command the same kind of loyalty from them.

If Mara didn't kill me first.

# CHAPTER 27

Steelbeard stood at the wheel day and night.

He had no need of sleep, unlike the rest of us. The men took turns at the wheel. He stayed with them, enjoying their company.

'There will be a storm the like of which you have never seen,' he warned. 'And when it seems that the ship is doomed, that she cannot possibly survive the winds, then we will know that we have found it.'

Nice.

Forewarned is fore-terrified. I really didn't like the sea. What was it they said? She was a harsh mistress?

'You won't be able to fight the storm. You are not meant to. Ride it out. At the first sight of storm clouds bring the man down from the crow's nest. No point losing a good man. Get him to look out for the thunderheads, not land. We sail directly into them. The storm will suck the ship in and draw us to the place we need to reach.' He looked at me then, a twinkle in his ghostly eye, and said, 'I just hope that you survive the journey.'

For some reason I hadn't considered the possibility that we might be in danger just *making* the voyage. It was one thing to go toe-to-toe with an all-powerful demon, the odds stacked impossibly in her direction, I made that choice willingly, it was just the way I rolled. But there was something entirely different about taking the men into a storm that could kill us all.

I could still feel the cold in my bones from the dead island. Nothing would drive it away. No heat was fierce enough to warm me. I sat in my cabin, waiting for the cry of 'Storm clouds!'.

I wrapped a blanket around myself to preserve the little heat I still had inside. It had been three days and I still hadn't shaken off the chill.

At last the bell sounded and men ran to the deck to brace the ship for the storm of the century. Everything had to be tied down or stowed away.

The ship turned towards the storm. It was madness. I

knew that in my heart of hearts. She was never built for this kind of manoeuvre. The mast strained with the effort of the turn. Salt spray stung our faces as waves thrashed against the hull.

And at last the rain was unleashed from the heavens.

'Lower the mainsails, brace the top sails!' MacLaine cried and ropes were released, whipping through the winches and pulleys as they dragged men across rain soaked decks until one of them tore free of the pirate's hands. The rope thrashed across the deck like an angry snake, then struck another deckhand, cracking a bone in his arm. His scream could be heard above the howl of the wind. MacLaine held onto the wheel, wrestling with the sea for control of it. 'You! Now! Help me lash this damn wheel!' He refused to leave his post and Steelbeard would never desert his old friend. The dead man would do everything he could to keep him safe, I knew that. One of the crew slipped and skidded across the soaked deck to help him tie down the wheel.

Below decks all we could do was brace ourselves in the corners as the ship rolled in the waves. The rolls became increasing violent as the ship was tossed by the storm. At times up seemed to become down and vice versa. Patty held onto me. I clutched her desperately. There was no weakness in it, every last man was petrified. This was the storm at its weakest. It was only going to get worse. The sheer elemental rage of it was terrifying.

Jaffar clutched at his knees. 'Gnomes aren't meant to go to sea,' he said over and over again.

Chani sat in absolute silence. She didn't resist the motion of the sea, seeming to become one with the ship. I saw her lips moving. She spoke an enchantment in whispered tones.

The main mast strained under the weight of the sails, made so much heavier by the rain. I thought it was going to tear free of its anchors, ripping the ship in two.

'Sail on! Into the eye of the hurricane!' I heard Steelbeard's maniacal cry.

It wasn't as though we could turn back.

This was it; we were the nautical equivalent of Garcia's desperate kill-or-be-killed lunge.

I couldn't help myself, I whispered a prayer. I didn't direct it to any god in particular. Anyone who felt like helping was fine by me.

The storm raged on.

The very skeleton of the ship screamed out, its timbers barely holding as the sea spilled in through widening leaks. And then I heard one huge earth-splitting crack and knew it was all over. The ship was going down.

The roaring stopped.

The storm was spent.

We were still alive.

Waves subsided and the ship fell to rest at last, the timbers almost offering a cheer of their own. We had sailed into the eye of the hurricane and come out the other side. Now we were becalmed. I heard Steelbeard give the command to run up the sails. Patty released her hold on me. Jaffar began to look a little less green. Chani had not changed her position during the entire storm-ravaged journey. She stopped chanting and finally opened her eyes. I had no idea if she had been trying to stop the storm, hold the ship together or calm her stomach.

Footsteps clattered along the corridor as pirates returned to the deck, ready to release MacLaine from his bindings and assess the damage.

I followed them.

MacLaine still stood at the wheel, his hands still clamped around it even though he was free of his bindings. Steelbeard still stood beside him. The storm hadn't touched the dead man, whereas MacLaine was soaked to the bone.

Neither man looked at me. They only had eyes for the Water Temple. It was a shimmering shape that seemed to float in the sea before us. Its colour changed and shifted with the motion of the sea, as though a part of the water itself rather than a solid structure on it.

I joined the pair of them at the wheel and marvelled at the impossible place.

We were being drawn towards it despite the sails being furled. There wasn't so much as a breath of breeze.

'She is calling to us,' Steelbeard said. 'Can't you hear her?'

All I could hear was the shushing of the sea as surf broke against the bow of the ship, but as I listened more intently I could hear a strange nagging *hum* that seemed to be just on the edge of hearing. There was little doubt that the sound was calling to us – calling or warning us not to approach.

We no longer had control over the ship.

'There will be creatures waiting. . . they will swarm the ship as we get closer. Have the artefacts ready. They are our only protection.'

In truth I had worn the amulet beneath my shirt from the moment he had given it to me. I didn't doubt for a moment that it had already protected me through a dozen misadventures. I was still alive, after all. I'd seen the power of the Harpoon myself, and experienced the deathly magic of the Bone Hand, but what of the Sacrificial Knife? What could that do? And how together could these four things help me destroy Mara?

The water between the ship and the temple began to bubble and boil. 'Down there! I swear I saw movement in the water!' Someone else cried, 'Mermaids!' and half the crew ran to the front of the ship. Oh, that it had really been mermaids come to sing their siren song and lure us to a watery grave in their lover's embrace. I could have died with that. But these things were not the stuff of any sailor's fantasies.

'Don't look down. Don't look back. Don't listen to them.' Steelbeard issued the orders, every inch the captain of our doomed vessel. The first of the monsters leapt salmon-like from the water, thrashing in the air. It reached, clawing at the planking. Wicked talons gouged into the wood, digging deep grooves into the hull. Those talons would slice through flesh like razors.

I hauled a man back from the edge. I could feel something was wrong. I don't know if it was the last lingering touch of death on me, the amulet or something else, but I could *feel* them weaving an enchantment about the ship.

I had to break it.

But how?

I held out the Harpoon. I couldn't shoot each and every one of them, but perhaps if I levelled a shot into the water it would spread out through the waves like lightning, frying them all?

Before I could, the first of the creatures touched the harpoon. It had no effect on the mass of skin and scales, teeth and claws. The creature leapt from the waves. Another tried to snatch it from my grasp. I held firm. The harpoon was useless. I might as well have used my sword on them.

Chani stepped in front of me. These things – maybe they were sirens, after all? Maybe that was the spell they were weaving, creating beauty for themselves? – had no effect on her. She watched them calmly. 'Rope,' she said after a moment. 'They cannot bear the touch of rope.'

'Do we have a fishing net?' I asked MacLaine. If anyone would know, he would. He'd memorised every item we carried on board the ship, I swear. A man of few words, he answered by opening a hatch and pulling out a loosely woven net. I wanted to kiss his ugly mug.

I took one corner of the net and made sure that MacLaine had another firmly in his grasp, but before we could cast it over the side one of the creatures leapt up the side of the ship and slashed at my arm. The skin turned red in a heartbeat. The creature crashed down into the sea below.

I ignored the pain. I could hurt later.

We dropped the net over the side and tied off our corners.

If Chani was wrong we were screwed. I trusted her. But I couldn't help imagining them streaming up the side of the ship using the netting as a ladder.

Chani was right. I don't know how she knew, what it was she'd seen, but the moment the rope netting landed on the creatures they screamed – and I mean *screamed* – with agony. Their flesh smouldered and sizzled and smoked, threatening to burst into flames.

So many of them were trapped between the net and the ship's hull, unable to escape from the torture the fibre was inflicting on them. It was slaughter. Mercifully their screams did not last long.

I didn't stay to watch them suffer.

I needed to bandage my arm before we reached the Temple.

The ship came to a sudden jarring halt as we reached our destination, trapping the last of Mara's minions between the hull and the Temple wall.

I didn't shed any tears for them, roles reversed they wouldn't have cried for me. I steeled myself to enter the Temple. I had wanted to go in with only Steelbeard for company, but Patty and Chani were not about to be left behind. Hell's teeth, even Jaffar stood at the ready.

'Maybe my name's waiting in there?' he said, with a wink. I could only assume the name he was looking for was 'victim', but he wouldn't be dissuaded.

MacLaine, too, was adamant that he was coming with us. I wasn't about to fight him, but Steelbeard wouldn't allow it. 'We need you out here, my old friend. Do this for me.' MacLaine relented.

So the five of us disembarked.

It wasn't long before we were inside the Water Temple and in the clutches of the many-tentacled demon that really wanted to hug the life out of us.

It wasn't as romantic as it sounded.

# CHAPTER 28

This is where we came in. Right back to the beginning of this little tale of mine – which of course is actually the *end* of this little tale of mine. But you needed to know how we got into this mess. Now you do. The whole sorry story.

They say your life flashes before your eyes. I guess it's true, in a way.

Mara squeezed like a bitch. I could barely draw half a breath, let alone a full one. She had one armed pinned by my side, crushing the life out of me. I clung onto the Titan Harpoon for grim death with my other hand.

It was the only thing I knew that could destroy her. Drop it and it was all over. She recognised it too. The tentacle that gripped me lifted me high in the air, then lashed about, twisting and turning me sickeningly. Up was down and down was up and I was going to lose my lunch, and my breakfast, and the quart of rum I'd downed for courage if I wasn't careful.

I caught a glimpse of Patty – beautiful, courageous Patty – standing toe-to-tentacle, slashing and hacking for all she was worth, her sword a silver web of brutal death – it moved so incredibly quickly, blurring in the air, but that wasn't what made it a web, it was the fact that once you were in it, snared, Patty would take your head off like a Black Widow. She sliced through black flesh. The tentacles continued to squirm and writhe on the temple floor even after they'd been severed.

Mara screamed – and there was nothing ladylike about it – as the pain of amputation tore through her oleaginous flesh. In answer, she squeezed even tighter. I felt my ribs beginning to crack. The stress on them was incredible. Blinding.

I tried desperately to shout, to call out, to tell Patty to stop, please, for the love of. . . well, for the love of me, frankly, but I couldn't draw enough air into my lungs to make anything even approaching a whisper.

Mara lashed out with the stump of the injured tentacle, black blood oozing from it. I think I was hallucinating from the lack of blood making it all the way to my head, but I could have sworn I saw it re-grow the tip that Patty had severed.

I tried to free myself from her clutches. I should have learned a thing or two from watching Jaffar wriggle out of Patty's grasp, but I only succeeded in tearing my shirt open as I struggled against her grip, revealing the Earth Amulet nestled against my chest. My heart was hammering. My head was spinning. I couldn't breathe. Spots of light cascaded across my one good eye. I was in trouble.

I smelt salvation rather than saw it; the moment that the Amulet came into contact with one of the suckers, Mara's cursed flesh turned into smoking liquid. And it reeked. The stuff of her flesh stung tears from my eye. I leaned into her embrace like some twisted lover enjoying the pain, and the Amulet fell against more of her body. The effect was the same. Mara's grip slackened, only slightly, but there was mercy in that little easing of the pressure on my body. She thrashed wildly, tentacles lashing at the air. There was no relief for her. And quite frankly I was glad about it. You can't exactly reason with a demoness.

I wormed my way out of her tentacular clutches and fell. It was further to the ground than I'd realised, otherwise I wouldn't have been quite so eager to break free until I was a bit lower. l dropped the Harpoon as I hit the ground.

The Titan weapon skidded away from me as I scrabbled out, trying to reach it. It was almost beneath her. It was well beyond my reach.

Not good. Not good at all.

All sorts of pain receptors fired off inside my body, but I couldn't afford even a heartbeat to acknowledge them or I might never get up. Maybe that's what makes a hero? When your body is beaten to a pulp, when there's no chance, you *still* get back up again? Or maybe that's what makes an idiot.

I launched myself at Mara, taking her in an embrace of my own.

I pressed the Amulet against her flesh.

Her razor-sharp teeth snapped and bit, only inches from my face: she had the worst case of morning-after breath I'd ever encountered. It was almost impossible to breathe through the stink of it. The incredible pain the Earth Amulet caused her prevented Mara from taking advantage of my nearness to finish me off.

I clung on while she thrashed about.

Finally, she dislodged me, but not until the damage had been done.

I fell backwards, rolling away. I felt a shooting pain from my shoulder, reminding me thoughtfully of just how much damage I'd put it through since becoming a pirate. Mara's howl was purely animalistic. It echoed throughout her prison, caught by the walls and amplified and turned back on her, as though the Temple shared her agony. The walls vibrated with the sound of her cries.

She was in no state to come at me.

A great swathe of flesh had burned away, exposing the demonic heart beating at her core.

There was no time like the present to get myself killed once and for all.

Everything hurt.

I risked a glance at Patty, and Chani and at little Jaffar, who'd crept forward now the tide seemed to have turned, and was going up against the stump of an amputated tentacle. And finally at Steelbeard, who nodded.

I rushed forward again, Sacrificial Knife in my fist. I hadn't realised I'd drawn it. It felt good in my hand, perfectly weighted despite its primitive design. Mara backed away like a frightened animal, her spirit broken. She knew why I was here. She knew what these artefacts meant, and like any frightened animal she did not want to die.

As she retreated I made a move for the Titan Harpoon, skidding across the water-slick tiles on my knees to snatch it up. The weapon came alive in my hands. It *knew*. It was ready. It had always been ready. Unlike me.

I braced myself to take aim, then drove the weapon deep into her. I came up onto my feet, putting all of my strength behind the blow and pinned Mara to the wall, driving the harpoon deeper and deeper, through her, into the very fabric of the temple, again and again, until at last she stopped moving. I didn't let go of the harpoon until the last of her tentacles fell limply to the ground, lifeless.

And then the agony and exhaustion of the months of pirate life hit me like a tidal wave. I was alive. I started to laugh, aware it sounded slightly hysterical in the confines of the legendary temple. I didn't care. I was alive.

I hauled myself back to my feet and turned to face the others.

I slipped the knife into my belt. I couldn't stop smiling. It felt *good* to be alive.

Jaffar was slumped in a corner. I don't know how he had got there. The last I'd seen he'd been killing an amputated tentacle. Chani knelt over him. I heard the gnome complaining loudly enough to know nothing was seriously wrong with him. Patty's sword arm hung limply at her side. I looked at her. She was barely able to retain her grip on her weapon. She was sprayed with Mara's blood, looking like someone's vision of a demoness herself, but she was alive. She'd never looked more beautiful to me.

I limped towards her. All I wanted to do was wrap my arms around her and say, 'I know we're not dead yet, but I have cleaned my teeth, so how about that kiss?' Her expression changed suddenly, as though she'd read my mind and was about to slap the notion out of it before I got carried away with myself.

It took a heartbeat to realise that she was looking at something over my shoulder.

I spun around on my heel.

Mara was still alive.

She had extricated herself from the Harpoon and was charging – or rather falling – towards me. Her blackened heart still beating inside the exposed cavity of her chest.

I'd forgotten about the one artefact that had not yet been used, but of course it had always had a purpose. It was made to kill. I pulled the Sacrificial Knife from my belt and without thinking, instinctively stepped into the demoness's wild, flailing reach, and plunged it directly into her heart. I held onto the hilt as the flint bled her out, until the diseased organ finally stopped beating.

Mara was gone. She had become the final sacrifice made in this place.

It was as though her life-force was little more than air and water. As she bled onto the temple floor she diminished, shrinking with each moment that passed.

I stood over her until she was all but washed out.

I felt rather than saw Steelbeard's ghost beside me. 'She gave you the artefacts to keep them as far as possible from her as she could, didn't she?' The ghost said nothing. 'They could all hurt her in some way. She wanted them in the hands of people she controlled.' I turned to face him. 'She just hadn't banked on you being able to resist her. You're the real hero, here.' Steelbeard still didn't say anything. He simply watched as Mara became less and less, until her corpse was little more than a stain on the wet floor.

I had no way of proving any of it, of course. But that didn't matter. The victors wrote history and today I was one of them, so that's exactly what the story would become.

'We'll make a pirate worthy of my daughter out of you yet, lad,' Steelbeard said.

'I wouldn't count on it,' I said, still smiling. 'That woman's far too good for me.'

'I won't argue with you there.'

We still had the harpoon, so we could destroy the Kraken but I suspected we wouldn't be seeing it again.

There was only one thing that remained.

This place needed to be sealed up, or better still, destroyed, in case Mara had left anything which would allow her power to be used by anyone – or anything – ever again.

# EPILOGUE

W ord spread like wildfire throughout the Southern
Seas; there was to be a conclave in Antigua.
A new order was rising in the wake of the deaths of
the old Pirate Captains. The tide was turning. Things
were changing.

Newcomers were trying to claim leadership of the
Pirate Brotherhood.

Uncertainty led to fear. Fear led to danger. And these
were already dangerous people. It wasn't a good state of
affairs. Without consensus there would be in-fighting.
There would be deaths.

The harbour bristled with masts. They were bare of
sails. They'd been taken down for repair. Every single
one of us knew this wasn't going to be a quick fix. It was
smart to make use of the downtime to carry out some

running repairs. If the Inquisition got wind of the conclave they could decimate the pirate fleet at a single stroke had they wanted to, even with their Kraken-depleted navy.

Speaking of which, there had been no news of the Kraken for weeks; no reports of it having attacked other ships, no sightings in open water. Free of Mara's control, its urge to destroy had almost certainly disappeared with it into the deepest and darkest waters. It would take years for the Inquisition to rebuild its fleet. That gave us years of freedom. The Southern Seas were ours. But the pickings were getting decidedly slim. Merchant shipping was down, cargoes worth picking over becoming fewer and further between. This really wasn't the time for us to be arguing amongst ourselves. Someone needed to drum that message home.

Surprisingly, we were not the only Inquisition ship flying the skull and crossbones, but people were still wary. Initially, it had been Steelbeard that had convinced the other captains we weren't still with the Inquisition, but it didn't take long before the one-eyed ex-Inquisitor was the talk of the other crews.

Honestly, I've never sought out fame. I've never been a glory hound. I'm just an ordinary guy who seems to find himself in the middle of extraordinary situations.

And then I go and do something stupid like trying to save the world because there's no one else around to do it. I just wanted to find a nice girl, settle down, have kids and enjoy my old age. Somehow, I didn't think that was going to happen.

'It looks like every damned pirate in the Southern Seas is here,' MacLaine observed.

'Well, at least one of them,' Steelbeard joked. Perhaps understandably, Patty didn't find his mortality jokes particularly amusing.

MacLaine dropped the anchor and the ship drifted to a halt.

All the men wanted to go ashore with me, but we didn't want to send the wrong signals to the parlay. The last thing I wanted was people thinking I was trying to give some sort of show of strength or muscle in on their territory. So, I had MacLaine pick an honour guard for me.

We arrived at the gathering in the harbour square just in time.

The crews of every ship had gathered together. The atmosphere was tense. The mass of so many men, and so many of them fuelled by rum, leant an edge of pent up aggression to the air. Steelbeard seemed to feel right at home in the middle of it. Men stepped aside for him when they almost certainly wouldn't have for me. We made our way towards the front. There was an argument taking place. It wasn't really a debate. That's implying a social etiquette to the happenings. This was a flat out argument. Voices cut across each other. Sentences were left half-heard, half-finished.

'This is a joke!'

'We need to appoint someone to act as our figurehead, now! It has to be someone we can all trust!'

'We have lost too many good men lately, honourable men that we all looked up to, but now they have all gone. Steelbeard, Crow and Garcia, we need someone like them.'

I half-expected to hear the ghost rumble: 'You can still have me.' But he stayed remarkably silent.

'Not *all* of the great captains are dead,' a voice cried out. A familiar figure started to mount the platform.

'Slayne!' I cursed my big mouth. I hadn't intended to say his name. It just came out. A few of the men around me took it up as a chant. 'Slayne! Slayne!'

'Friends,' he said, raising his hands like some damned messiah. 'Most of you know me and those who don't almost certainly know *of* me. I am a man of my word.

You all know that. So when I say I am the man best able to lead the Brotherhood, believe me, I *am* the best man to lead the Brotherhood!'

A cheer went up from the crowd. I looked around at the faces. The most noise came from the younger pirates, new bloods, rather than the older wily souls who actually knew Slayne. He was trading purely on his reputation as being a hard man. A man who got what he wanted. I started to turn away, prepared to head back to the ship and be done with this lot of fools. I wasn't a joiner. I'd learned that the hard way with the Inquisition. I'd happily let them all get into bed with Slayne, it didn't bother me one way or the other. It wasn't like I had to sail with him.

I hadn't got five paces when I heard Steelbeard cry: 'He's a liar and a coward!' I turned to see the dead man climbing up onto the platform to confront Slayne. My first thought was: *this can't be good*. My second was: *but it could be fun*. My third was: *oh hell, he's looking at me*. 'You know me, brothers. I may be dead, but that does not change the truth as I speak it! This man has betrayed his brothers! This man is not to be trusted! Not at any cost!' He beckoned me to join him. I really didn't want to.

'He left this man, the captain of my former crew, and my only daughter, to die after trapping them!'

'He was trying to steal from me!' Slayne wheedled.

'No!' Steelbeard roared. 'He was not! He was following my *orders*!' That had everyone's attention. Two pirate captains going up against each other? Every single man in the crowd was quiet now. 'He was retrieving an artefact that belonged to your mistress, Slayne. Yes! This great pirate captain was under the influence of another, nothing more than a glorified lackey for the sea demon, Mistress Mara, or did you call her Lady, Slayne? Mara, the demoness who unleashed the Kraken on ships that should have been ours for the taking! He destroyed our livelihoods for his own personal gain! He is nothing but a servant of the damned!'

A ripple of murmurs passed through the crowd as pirate turned to pirate, the news infecting them like a sickness.

'But this man destroyed her! This man, this *hero*, has made the seas safe for us again!'

I could have killed him if he wasn't already dead.

The murmur was replaced by a cheer. 'Who should be your leader? Not the man who could have destroyed you!'

Cries of 'Aye!' went up.

I looked out at a sea of faces. They didn't know me.

How could they really want me to be their leader? I was an outsider. . .

'He's not one of us,' Slayne objected. 'He is an Inquisition man!'

He drew his sword and was upon me before my hand had even touched the hilt of my own.

Steelbeard stepped between us.

Slayne's blade passed straight through him. It drew a deep intake of breath from the crowd. Stunned shock. Steelbeard's action was purely instinctive. If he hadn't already been dead it *would* have cost him his life. Mortality – or immortality – aside, his defence caused Slayne to half-pull his blow and bought me the room I needed to get out of the way. There was nothing gracious about my evasion. I tripped over my own feet, and fell, coming down on that damaged shoulder. I didn't have a choice. I tried to turn the fall into a roll, and somehow ended up taking Slayne's legs out from under him in the process. I'm not sure what it must have looked like from the crowd, but there wasn't a single intentional move in it.

I came up onto my feet, sword in hand, ready to defend myself. Slayne stared at me, eyes blazing with pure hatred. I have no idea if he even realised he'd just turned the entire pirate nation against him in one single move. If he did, he didn't let this slow him down. This was all about killing me for his personal satisfaction now. It had nothing to do with claiming leadership of the Brotherhood.

I could respect that, but I didn't have to like it. And I didn't intend to let him have the satisfaction either, mind you. I parried the next stroke and the next. He was easy to read. His body telegraphed every swing and not-so subtle feint long before they came. He was attacking with pure anger in his heart. And that was what killed him, long before my sword did. I didn't say a word. Didn't goad him. Didn't even really *fight* him. I kept my distance, light on my feet, dancing just out of the reach of his wild attacks as they became more and more frantic.

He was out of control.

I realised then that I'd misjudged things.

He was dangerous.

I barely managed to push his arm away from me as the blow slipped past my guard.

It was less than an inch from showing the crowd the contents of my last meal, and making it quite literally my last meal. But lady luck was smiling broadly right then; I caught my heel on a loose piece of planking on the platform, turning my ankle. I stumbled a step to the side. It saved my life. It also completely unbalanced Slayne as he'd thought for sure his thrust had done the trick, but with nothing to slow the blow he staggered forward. He was too close for the sword now. This was my kind of fight. I threw my elbow up into his face, connecting with his nose and driving it back into his head. He stumbled, dazed. The crowd roared its approval. I followed up with a crunching right hook, and as his head snapped back, I stepped in, driving my knee into his balls. He went down like a sack of potatoes.

They were roaring now, the rum fuelling the cheers.

I faced the crowd.

I didn't know whether to bow or apologise for ruining their assembly.

My indecision nearly made it all the more memorable because Slayne wasn't done with me.

Well, by the time I turned around he was. But there was a split second when things could have been oh so different. Someone cried a warning. I didn't understand it for one deathly moment, then realised too late what it meant. I spun around on my heel, ready to throw my hands up to ward off his killer blow, only to see Patty standing over the corpse, her knife embedded deep in

Slayne's neck.

'This is where you kiss me,' she said.

I took the hint.

It wasn't all that long ago I was an Inquisition man through and through. Well, there was some wine in there too, obviously. But that was all the stuff of the dim and disaffected distant past. I had a new life. I had Patty at my side. I could do anything.

Chants of 'Captain! Captain!' went up. Every single voice in the crowd took up the cry.

I turned to Steelbeard's grinning spectre. I shook my head. I really didn't want to be a bloody hero. Not again.

'I don't think it's your choice, lad. The people have spoken.'

'More fool the bloody people, then.'

Patty said, 'My hero.'

On second thoughts, who was I to argue with the people?

**THE END**